The lagoon they walked along was a magical sight.

"This has been lovely, Georgia," Link murmured, "but I can only resist you for so long."

For a moment her head reeled at the note in his voice. His hands were locked at her waist, holding her lightly but firmly, discovering all of a sudden she was trembling.

"Georgia?" he prompted in a low voice.

Such a shock of desire ran through her she broke away as though burned.

"You'll have to catch me first!" she called in a kind of defiance over her shoulder.

"Done."

She had a few yards' start and she was very fleet of foot. She was running as though from an explosive situation. Running as though scared of her own sensuality. And in her twenty-four years only Link had unlocked it.

Dear Reader,

It is with pleasure, pride and a sense of personal achievement that I join in congratulating Harlequin on forty years of luminous Romance. In that time Harlequin has developed the genre into an art form able to express the hopes and dreams of countless thousands of women across the world. Harlequin Romance provides quality stories full of enjoyment, comfort, travel, color and that little bit of magic women must have in their lives. On a personal note twenty-five years on in my career, Harlequin has given me the nearly perfect way to make a living and the wonderful opportunity of becoming a roving ambassador for my own country, Australia.

I remember myself as a little girl forever scribbling in my endless notebooks. I often wondered if anyone would ever read a word I said. Harlequin certainly helped me achieve that, and I am grateful!

I hope you enjoy my celebratory offering, *Georgia and the Tycoon*, and I take this opportunity to thank Harlequin and my loyal readership for their support.

May Romance continue to blossom forever in our hearts.

Margaret Way

Georgia and
the Tycoon
Margaret Way

Harlequin Books

TORONTO • NEW YORK • LONDON
AMSTERDAM • PARIS • SYDNEY • HAMBURG
STOCKHOLM • ATHENS • TOKYO • MILAN
MADRID • WARSAW • BUDAPEST • AUCKLAND

ISBN 0-373-03455-5

GEORGIA AND THE TYCOON

First North American Publication 1997.

Copyright © 1997 by Margaret Way.

All rights reserved. Except for use in any review, the reproduction or
utilization of this work in whole or in part in any form by any electronic,
mechanical or other means, now known or hereafter invented, including
xerography, photocopying and recording, or in any information storage
or retrieval system, is forbidden without the written permission of the
publisher, Harlequin Enterprises Limited, 225 Duncan Mill Road,
Don Mills, Ontario, Canada M3B 3K9.

All characters in this book have no existence outside the imagination of
the author and have no relation whatsoever to anyone bearing the same
name or names. They are not even distantly inspired by any individual
known or unknown to the author, and all incidents are pure invention.

This edition published by arrangement with Harlequin Books S.A.

® and TM are trademarks of the publisher. Trademarks indicated with
® are registered in the United States Patent and Trademark Office, the
Canadian Trade Marks Office and in other countries.

Printed in U.S.A.

CHAPTER ONE

"Excuse me," Georgia said sweetly, grabbing for the rear door handle of the taxi and holding on for dear life.

"*My* cab, I think." He regarded her very coolly, his vibrant voice abrasive, conveying a fine disregard for long-stemmed blondes who demanded equal rights on the one hand and all the old female perks on the other.

"How do you fathom that?" It came out with just the right note of wide-eyed astonishment.

"Try, I was here *first*."

Georgia looked at him in some consternation, discovering he was in his early thirties, very tall, strongly built, impeccably tailored. So close to, she could see the fine grain of his tawny gold skin, the sheen of his black hair and the way his thick black eyelashes curved away from remarkable light eyes. He was certainly very handsome but of a type she had always disliked. The corporate dynamo. The decision maker. The power broker. Someone, in fact, like her father.

"As far as I'm concerned our race was a dead heat," she pointed out fairly. "Maybe your hand touched down first, but that's only because you have a much longer arm." Long used to male indulgence, the last thing Georgia had expected was coming up against a brick wall.

"Why don't you just admit it. You expected me to back off."

5

Sparks flew around them, but still Georgia tried one of her melting smiles. They usually worked. "Look," she confided, "I'm running late and I have a *plane* to catch."

"Of course you do." His tone was crisp. "It so happens, so do I."

Damn! No sign of a breakthrough. He wasn't getting into the spirit of things at all.

"What's it to be, folks?" the taxi driver called. "There are a lot of hysterical people right behind you on the pavement."

"Sharing's fine." Georgia made the bright suggestion.

"Why don't you get in then." He looked down his arrogant straight nose at her. One saw them on Roman statues.

Georgia made a point of smiling sweetly. "Thank you *so* much," she said with exaggerated politeness. She ducked her blonde head, half wanting to tell the taxi driver to take off. At least the wretched man didn't try to sit beside her. He swung into the front seat beside the driver, very lithe and coordinated.

"Domestic, international?" he asked, giving her a brief searing backward glance. Or was that the eyes? They were grey. But shatteringly bright. Some might even call them silver. Not *pure* silver, of course. But close enough.

"Domestic, thank you," Georgia replied coolly, smoothing her long gleaming hair and looking out the window. "The Ansett terminal."

"Ansett for me, too," he told the driver as though further irritated by the fact they shared a destination.

Georgia moved closer to the window feigning interest

in the swirling noonday crowds. What an objectionable man. He made her feel like a no-account social butterfly flitting madly all over town when she was a career woman with her own successful business.

She worked hard. Harder than any of her staff. *Too* hard, according to her doctor. Only a few weeks before, her immune system had temporarily gone on the blink when she came down with a severe case of winter flu. She hadn't recovered with her usual speed or vitality. On top of that she had broken up with Gavin. Gavin was a trial lawyer, a good one. But he'd brought his court-room tactics to bear on her once too often. Most of the time he was just plain jealous. As there hadn't been any kind of basis for his histrionics, she'd thought it time to call it off. Not that it was really *working*. Gavin kept showing up with all kinds of displays of his affection. She was tired of sending back the flowers.

Up front the dynamo and the taxi driver were having an in-depth discussion about the China crisis. Deng Xiaoping. Who would fill the power vacuum. Both of them seemed to know a lot about it. When they got around to Hong Kong Georgia thought she might have something to offer but didn't feel like risking another one of those mind-bending stares. The minutes were ticking away, and she felt in danger of missing her plane. Not that it would be a catastrophe. She could simply fax Uncle Robert to say she'd been delayed.

Robert Mowbray was her mother's only brother and Georgia's godfather. It was he who had suggested she recuperate on Sunset, the tropical resort he owned and ran on that glorious Great Barrier Reef island. Just to think of Sunset was to have an instant vision of peacock blue skies, palm-fringed white beaches and a sparkling turquoise sea of incredible translucence. A few weeks of sea and sunshine, delicious food and exploring the breathtaking coral gardens should restore her in mind and body. She would be company for Uncle Robert, too, since he lost Dee, his adored wife and partner of thirty years. The whole family found it hard to believe Dee had gone. She had been such a bright, energetic person and wonderfully competent. Uncle Robert would be missing her dreadfully not only as his dearest friend and life's companion but as his partner in the business. There had been plans to build a nine-hole golf course on Sunset but without Dee it hadn't happened. Dee had always been full of life. Full of plans.

When she came out of her poignant thoughts Georgia saw to her relief they were clear of the city and into the suburbs. The two up front were now discussing big game fishing. Why didn't they stick to the really important things in life? To the extent she was trapped and had no place else to look she was struck by the attractiveness of the back of the dynamo's head. Not every man had such a shapely head or that smooth golden nape. She glanced away quickly. The sooner they were at the airport the better. She had more important things to do than study a man's nape with fevered attention.

Fifteen minutes later they arrived, splitting the fare. *Exactly*. Right down the middle. Not a cent more or a cent less. At over six feet *he* had to fend for himself, but a porter charged to Georgia's assistance. She smiled as he loaded her two pieces of luggage. By the time they made it to the counter, the dynamo was there before her. A tall, indeed dominating figure in the queue. Their shared destination was a leading tourist town in North Queensland and a point of departure for several of the Barrier Reef resorts. A detail that annoyed her.

With any luck at all he would be going to Hayman, an international five-star. Sunset, though physically very beautiful with an extensive fringing reef and good accommodation, was considerably down-market from Royal Hayman.

In the boarding lounge Georgia sat as far away from the dynamo as she could. Something about him endangered her psyche. That striking appearance and vibrant voice didn't fool her. Men like that were rather more trouble than they were worth. Her father, a top businessman, though indulgent in his fashion, had never taken her mother seriously since the day they were married. There had been no sign he was going to take Georgia seriously, either, until the day she'd left home. So much for controlling males. Males for whom *the job* came first.

Georgia took a seat, crossing her legs. There were people everywhere. The flight had been fully booked. While the southern states of Australia still shivered, Queensland was paradise, especially north of Capricorn. Most of the passengers wore colourful resort clothes, obviously heading for the islands. To her right several young women were chattering excitedly about all the attractive guys they were going to meet. It didn't necessarily have to happen, Georgia thought, but she wished them well. One of the girls confessed in a very forthright, open way she had invested her last dollar on a fabulous wardrobe in the hope of catching a rich husband. Georgia was startled. It didn't sound in the least *romantic*. Besides, were there any millionaires left on the market? Surely most had been snatched up. For the third or fourth time, Georgia reflected she had met a tall, dark and handsome stranger in the past *hour*. From the way he looked and dressed he had money, as well, but all *she* had felt was hostility. It wasn't just that his type reminded her of her father. It was *personal*. A man-woman thing. Merely thinking about it made her direct a quick glance towards the far end of the room. At that moment the dynamo looked up from the open pages of the *Financial Review* to smile at a passing air hostess, a young woman he apparently knew. It was a smile of heart-stopping charm, quirky, sexy, white teeth against a tanned skin. It even had a real warmth in it. Georgia almost clicked her tongue in amazement. Obviously he wasn't as grim as she'd thought.

She turned back, realising in the next second this was going to be her day for incidents. A plump toddler with a fuzz of fiery curls, his face and hands covered in chocolate, made a staggering beeline for her, knowing, in the way children did, Georgia loved kids. Ordinarily she would have handled the situation easily, perhaps got into conversation, but she was dressed from head to toe in pristine summer white, a designer shirt and matching linen trousers.

Georgia stood up hurriedly, but despite her evasive action there was no sign of parental intervention until the very last moment, when the child's father seized the boy up with a loud, "Ha, Josh! Mustn't put chocky on the lovely lady."

Josh roared his protest but was carried away nonetheless. There were plenty of witnesses to the little incident, including the dynamo, who gave Georgia another one of his high-intensity glances, this time spiked with undeniable black humour. It was obvious he had written her off as one of those vain creatures who lived in constant fear of having her outfits ruined. Georgia flicked her long hair away from her nape and resumed her seat, feeling a tingle of heat in her face. She realised she was taking this man a lot more seriously than he deserved. But then he appeared to be keeping a rather sharp eye on *her*. Maybe her father had sent him. It wasn't impossible. Though her father was fairly careful to keep his inquiries discreet, he had never stopped keeping tabs on her. The worst time had been when he hid himself in the back of her car.

All for nothing. She'd had absolutely no intention of going away with Gavin for the weekend. Her father had neither liked nor approved of Gavin, which may have been part of his attraction. That, and he closely resembled the American actor James Spader.

Georgia was busy writing a little note for herself when a male voice called, "Georgia, darling!"

It was an open display of affection in a public place. At least fifty people looked up, including the girls, who collectively sat forward.

"Gavin." Georgia felt a lurch of dismay.

"Darling." He flopped into the seat beside her, puffing slightly because he'd needed to run. "Trish told me only an hour ago you were off to Sunset. I just jumped in the car and drove straight here. Risked a fine, as well. Something I don't need."

"Trish will be hearing from me," Georgia murmured, feeling betrayed.

"If you don't ask, you'll never know," Gavin told her with a grin. "Actually poor old Trish told me before she even realised what she'd said. I don't know why you keep her on. She's as thick as a brick."

"She doesn't have much to do with trial lawyers," Georgia said tartly. "Anyway, no one, absolutely *no one* makes better curtains, cushions, bedspreads, things like that."

"Hell, I didn't come here to talk about Trish," Gavin said, looking around at his captive audience much as he did in court. He reached out and touched Georgia's long hair, running a caressing hand down its long, shining length. "So, why all the secrecy, princess?"

Georgia raised her delicate brows. "Since you ask, it's no longer any of your business. We split up, remember?" Gently but firmly she pulled away.

Gavin looked into her eyes soulfully. "We didn't split up, my darling. you simply *panicked*. You've been ill, though you're starting to look your old gorgeous self. You're overworked. God knows *why*, when your father would give you everything you want on a silver platter. The job got on top of you. It *can* happen. We're still best friends, aren't we?"

"Sorry, no. But I suppose we could be friendly again one of these days." Georgia sighed. "I need space."

Gavin laughed. "You're lying to me, doll. So tell me, how long do you intend to stay?"

"At least a couple of years."

"I could do with a break myself," Gavin said slowly, thoughtfully.

"Sunset is absolutely full up." Georgia shook her

head. "I have it from Uncle Robert they're camping out on the balconies."

"I don't think so, Georgia," Gavin said with an unblinking look. "Word is Sunset's not getting the bookings these days."

"A temporary thing." Georgia felt sad. "Uncle Robert is missing Dee frightfully."

"It can't be easy," Gavin said. "What he really ought to do is sell."

"That's out of the question. Sunset is Uncle Robert's life."

Gavin stared at her for a moment, his good-looking face expressionless. "That's rather a dumb thing to say, Georgie, and you're far from dumb."

"Have you heard something I haven't?" she challenged.

"I like to get a line on all your family, princess. Your Uncle Robert's in a few financial straits. Surely you know that?"

"Nothing he can't get out of," Georgia said heatedly. "Why don't you mind your own business, Gavin, instead of running around like a private detective."

"I don't have to run around, hon," he said casually. "I simply have to pick up the phone. Investigating is part of my job. Anyway, look what I've got you." He reached into his breast pocket and withdrew a small velvet box.

"No!" Georgia began to shake her head, realising what was coming.

"You haven't seen it yet." Gavin smiled complacently, opening it up and turning it towards her. "Three

months' salary. A full carat. For my one and only girl.''
He leaned forward and kissed her hungrily on the mouth.

"You expect us to become *engaged*?" Georgia said when she was able, desperately trying to keep her tone quiet.

"Sure, sweetie. I'm counting on it."

"I wouldn't have thought even *you* could be so thick-skinned." Anger was quickly overcoming Georgia's distaste for a public row.

"Georgie, I *know* you." Gavin's voice was pure courtroom. "You like to cover up your feelings. But you *love* me. I know you better than you know yourself." Before she could stop him Gavin pushed his ring on her finger as though the very action settled the matter.

"What a bully you are." Despite herself Georgia flapped the ring back and forth. It was a very nice ring, but she pulled it off her finger and tossed it lightly in the air. "I hope you kept your sales docket, because this is going back."

It was too much for the group to the right. "Isn't that *awful*!" one of the girls cried.

"Just awful! The poor guy."

"I'd never knock an engagement ring back myself," said a third.

Georgia began to wonder if they weren't going to make a chorus.

"You don't *mean* this, Georgie," Gavin protested, neatly pocketing the ring. "You're just into being your own woman for a while."

"Tell me about it." Georgia stood up determinedly as over the public address system the passengers were advised their flight was now boarding. "I have to go,

Gavin," she said. "Forgive me if I've hurt you but you had no right to pull a stunt like that."

Gavin's super confidence faded slightly, but characteristically he was unwilling to give up. "We've had our troubles, Georgie, but you love me. That's the point."

Georgia picked up her hand luggage. Gavin moved with her. "How could you do this to me, Gavin?" She felt she could hardly stand it.

"If I've upset you I'm sorry." The thing was he made it sound like an outright lie.

"You *know* we've split up yet you turn up here and propose. You got an audience, too, which is what you really love."

The passengers were all converging on the door and Georgia tensed as she realised the dynamo was regarding them with a considerable degree of irony in his sparkling eyes. Perhaps he had seen her toss Gavin's ring away. The little ceremony had scarcely been private.

"I'll say goodbye now, darling," Gavin said, beginning to draw her into his arms. "You'll be seeing me soon."

Georgia pulled away, hardening her voice. "I won't lie to you, Gavin. That would be a big mistake."

"You'll feel better after a week or two." He gave her a look of endless patience, but Georgia shook her head dismissively and turned away. With nothing left to say, Gavin shot a quick glance at the tall dynamic guy he knew from somewhere or other. He even gave an uncertain, "Hi!" searching his mind for details. The guy nodded but didn't speak.

A few moments later Georgia was walking across the tarmac trying to control her feelings of upset and frustration. Men were such strange creatures. Most of them viewed women as *property*. Under her cool she was perturbed about what Gavin might do. Take his stunt today. She had made it perfectly plain their affair was over no matter *what* he did. Persistence was one thing, but this was harassment, wasn't it? At least in her eyes. She had never told Gavin she loved him. She had never slept with him, although she couldn't count the times he had begged her to. What *had* she seen in him? He could be funny, good company. He was good-looking, clever, if overly opinionated. There wasn't the slightest doubt he loved having her on his arm, but he'd shown no interest whatsoever in her career. As far as he was concerned, it fell into the none-too-serious bracket.

There was a fairly brisk cross wind blowing. Georgia put a restraining hand to her streaming hair, only to be pulled up short. The ends were caught in something. What? She turned quickly, feeling another tiny tug of pain.

"Hang on a moment." The dynamo was looking at her with a hint of impatience. "A strand of your hair is caught in my sunglasses."

"Good heavens!" Her tone suggested he had engineered it.

"One of the hazards of having a long mane, I should think."

He was disturbingly close, his long, elegant fingers extracting a few shining strands from the section of raised gold on an arm of his expensive sunglasses. He must have been in the act of slipping them on or holding them up in the air.

"Caught like a nymph in a Greek legend," he said

mockingly, then with another little tug freed her. "Maybe a few split ends."

"I won't worry about that."

"And here *I* thought you wouldn't settle for less than perfection."

"Looking good is part of my job," Georgia said crisply. "Thanks anyway."

He continued to keep pace with her. "I seem to know your boyfriend. Would you mind telling me his name?"

"I don't pass out that sort of information to complete strangers."

"Come on," he said with a scoffing inflection. "I'm perfectly respectable."

"I've lost track of the number of tricksters who fit into that category."

"That's true." He sounded amused. "One can't be too careful. It's all right anyway. I've just remembered. Gavin Underwood, the barrister?"

"Yes, and you know what *that* means."

"No. Tell me."

"You wouldn't want to tangle with him."

"Really?" This time he laughed. "You don't seem to want to, either. You threw something. I couldn't quite figure out if it was a ring."

"A fake, if you're interested."

"It looked like a diamond ten rows away."

"Maybe he got it cheaply in Hong ˜ong. Anyway, why all the questions?"

"Just idle chatter. Besides, we seem to be seeing rather a lot of each other."

"Which is odd. I must have imagined your antisocial behaviour."

"I've no idea what you're getting at." He looked at her.

"I think you do. It crossed my mind at one point I'd have to fight you for the cab."

He gave a brief laugh. "My feelings of outrage have undergone a change. Strictly speaking it's not *your* fault. I expect you've been indulged since the days your brown eyes peeped out of a shawl."

"I have to admit to getting my fair share of notice," Georgia replied almost recklessly, "but I don't think it spoiled me."

"So I can't cite this afternoon?"

"No. I don't ordinarily fight over cabs, but I told you it was an emergency."

"Well, we got here." He shrugged lazily. "Don't worry about it."

"I'm trying hard not to." Georgia felt genuinely rattled. "Anyway, I think we're about to part company."

"I wouldn't be too sure of it," he commented lightly. "We're both forward. It's even possible we might sit together."

"I'm going first class." She knew in a split second so was he.

"I knew that the moment I laid eyes on you."

"Well, enjoy the trip." Georgia was surprised by her own turn of speed. This man was having an incredible effect on her. It wasn't often she lost her cool confidence, and she wasn't enjoying it.

A few minutes later, when she was comfortably settled on the plane, the air hostess paused beside her, as though she couldn't believe Georgia's luck.

"Yours is the window seat, Mr. Robards." She smiled brilliantly at the tall man just behind her.

"Thank you." The silvery eyes positively glittered. "You'd prefer the window seat, wouldn't you?" He addressed Georgia directly.

"I couldn't think of depriving you of it." Despite herself a powerful thrill spread through her.

"I insist."

"Very well." She wasn't about to press it. Robards. She knew that name.

"Please let me know if there's anything you want." The air hostess was still murmuring to him. Obviously she knew who he was. From his dark golden tan, he was probably a frequent commuter.

While he was settling himself Georgia glanced out the window, glad she had thought to bring a book, one of the courtroom genre she'd become addicted to. She even went so far as to take it out of her bag and settle it in the seat pocket in front of her. The last thing she needed was nearly three hours of highly charged conversation with the man beside her. It struck her she could fly to New Zealand in the time it took her to get from one end of Queensland to the other, and that left out the entire wilderness area of Cape York.

"Do you enjoy flying?" he asked, as they gathered speed for the takeoff.

"I can think of things I like better."

"Oh, Lord!"

The sarcasm again. "I have no intention of bothering *you*," she said coolly. "I'll call the hostess if a wing drops off."

"If you think she can help. Actually I spotted the hostility between us an hour or so back."

"And no improvement so far."

"Obviously you believe in giving it to a guy straight."

"I do, too." Georgia broke off to take a toffee the air hostess passed.

Moments later they were airborne, and the faint popping in her ears quickly stopped.

"There, that wasn't so bad." He gave her a brief sidelong smile.

"Landing is more dangerous," she pointed out. "Look, you don't *have* to talk to me. I have a book to read."

"You should have asked about it before you picked it up. I'd give it a four out of ten."

"Then there's a distinct possibility I'll enjoy it."

"I expect you like all that lawyer stuff because of Underwood?"

"Not at all," Georgia corrected him gently. "*Despite* him, I'd say. And you? Don't you have work to do? Where's your laptop?"

"I left it at home. I'm on holiday," he said lazily.

"Royal Hayman?"

"Not this time. I'm off to Sunset."

"Really?" she finally managed to say.

"So help me out. Where are *you* going? Not Sunset by any chance?"

"Actually, yes." She didn't tell him of the connection.

"Why so glum? I do hope it doesn't have anything to do with me."

"Don't be absurd!" She eased forward and withdrew the thick paperback from the seat pocket.

"I think this is a simple case of starting off badly."

"I won't argue." Pointedly Georgia turned to page one.

"I'm sure you'll guess who dunnit right off," he said, a sardonic sparkle in his crystal-clear eyes.

"Believe me, if *you* did, I will, too."

He laughed, the most attractive sound she'd heard in a long while.

It was a full fifteen minutes before he spoke to her again, during which time the same air hostess wandered up for a little husky chat. Georgia, who was supposed to be reading her book, understood he was a regular commuter, unmarried by the sound of it, and clearly regarded by the airline as a VIP. They were almost at the end of their conversation before it suddenly hit her.

Robards.

Why hadn't she thought of it before? Anyone in the hotel business would know the name. Sam Robards was an enormously successful hotel magnate. Not that there had to be any connection. Sam Robards would have to be in his sixties. The dynamo was thirty-one or thirty-two at the outside. Anyway, the Robards chain was confined to the major capital cities and several provincial towns. She had never heard any mention they had interests in the north.

A short time later another attendant arrived with lunch, which they both declined, settling for coffee.

"Watching the calories?" Georgia asked, as if she'd never seen anyone in worse shape.

"If I don't feel like it I don't eat." The silver-grey

eyes mocked her. "You look like someone with a passion for diet and the gym yourself."

"I try to stick to a very healthy regime. I work out but I don't have time to get down to the gym. Generally I run."

"I did notice your turn of speed," he said dryly. "May I ask what you *do*?"

She shook her head, then changed her mind. "I run a successful interior design business. What's your story?"

"What about names first?" he suggested. "I'm Link Robards."

"Georgia Bennett. How do you do?"

He leaned back indolently in the seat, studying her profile. "So you're a career woman?"

"Do you have a problem with that?" She flashed him a cool look.

"Hardly. Why so toey?"

"I expect it's because I've spent years leaping to my own defence."

"I wouldn't worry about it," he said in a sardonic voice. "It must have helped. You obviously thrive on a challenge."

"And I've decided *you're* a corporate dynamo."

"So who told you?" He lifted a mocking eyebrow.

"I've lived with one for most of my life."

"I take it you mean your father?"

Georgia nodded. "Much as I love him, he tried to thwart my ambitions at every turn."

"That must have been a frustrating experience," he said. "Your father's not Dawson Bennett, by any chance?"

"I was hoping you'd fill me in on *your* father,"

Georgia countered. "He's not Sam Robards, the hotel magnate?"

"I believe he has achieved that status."

"And you work for him, of course?"

"I'm right up there at the top," he said smoothly. "I have two sisters also in the family business, along with their husbands, a couple of uncles and several of my cousins. No one could accuse Dad of not being family-minded."

"And you never wanted to strike out on your own?" She knew her tone was too challenging, but he affected her that way.

He glanced at her in recognition, eyes narrowing. "There *was* a time." He paused, shrugging philosophically. "A few years out of university. An architect full of plans, but it all fell flat when my father had his first heart attack. He's had a triple bypass since, but it took quite a while before he was ready to raise hell again. His one request was for me to *be* there, to be ready to take over. In due course I will."

"But surely in your business you'd be able to use your skills as an architect?"

"To an extent," he agreed. "I have a lot of say. I do my own thing. I respect my father enormously, but we don't always agree."

"So why are you dropping in on Sunset?" Georgia asked, starting to feel uneasy.

"I'm not allowed to?" His eyes were as hard as diamonds.

"I thought being in the business you'd go for the top of the range."

"Not at all. Besides, I've seen Sunset. It may need a

major overhaul, but the island is very beautiful and so's the fringing reef. How come *you* picked it?''

Georgia gripped her book. ''I've been there several times, and I always want to go back. I'm wondering, though, if *you* have some ulterior motive?''

''You think you're entitled to know?'' He gave her another sharp look.

''It hardly matters, at this point. You know what they say. Strangers tend to confide in one another.''

Her words made him laugh. ''Mostly I don't tell anyone a *thing*! It has to be the flower eyes, soft and guileless as pansies. They should be at odds with your blonde hair but they're not. Don't tell me if you touch it up. I'd be terribly disappointed.''

''Not with anything more drastic than shampoo and conditioner,'' Georgia said. ''Hair and eye colour are my own.''

''So *are* you Dawson Bennett's daughter? You don't sound too sure.''

''For heaven's sake, of course I am.'' Georgia tossed her blonde hair. Something about him made her unbearably self-conscious. Aware of herself as a woman. ''He was certainly there when I was born,'' she said. ''He raised me. We've been arguing for years. I am, in fact, his only child.''

''It looks like he took extremely good care of you.''

Georgia nodded. ''But he has very archaic ideas about a woman's place.''

''You mean, find a comfortable easy job until you're married?''

''In my case not even as adventurous as that. According to Dad it's *his* job to take care of my mother and me. I didn't actually *need* a job. My mother spends all her time visiting art galleries and antique shops, having lunches, going shopping, playing bridge. Filling in the time.''

"I'm not too sure what to say to that," he remarked, understanding in his voice. "My mother does pretty much the same thing. Plenty of women in jobs might like to change places with them.''

"Well, I'm a little more ambitious than that," Georgia said, a sparkle in her eyes. "I like to use what talents I have.''

"Did you train before you became an interior designer?''

"Are you patronising me?" Georgia demanded, responding to the faint slash in his tone.

"Well, *yes*." His smile flashed like a bright light. "At least until you get rid of that chip on your shoulder.''

"Lord, I *know*! But I've had some funny things happen to me. I doubt they would have happened to a male colleague. To answer your question, I did a Fine Arts course at university and later I worked for Bobby St. George for a couple of years. You've heard of him, haven't you?''

"I have." His handsome mouth compressed. "As an architect I have to tell you I dislike his interiors. Over the top, if you like.''

"I don't love them, either," Georgia admitted, "but Bobby's an enthralling character. A professional through and through. He deserves to be at the top of the profession even if one doesn't go for knock-em-dead glamour.''

"I know a lot of better people than that," he said flatly.

"Well, you're going to be amazed to hear I won Young Designer of the Year when I was still with Bobby. The judges were very impressed with my use of colour, scale and detailing. They said I had a light, elegant hand."

"Thank God for that!" he said in a crisp voice.

"I can even go one better. I won Best Residential Interior last year. It was featured in at least two design and decorating magazines. Even my father sent out for copies."

"If you tell me the issue I'll have my staff search it out."

"I'm going back to my book," Georgia said disgustedly.

"Don't be like that. We're actually getting along rather well."

"Aside from the little gibes."

She was trying to find her page when the aircraft seemed to shudder then drop. Never the best of travellers, Georgia gave an involuntary little cry that abruptly cut out. She flailed in the air for something to hold onto, eventually settling on a strong supporting hand. She had never come to terms with hitting air pockets. Probably never would.

It was moments more before the aircraft levelled out, and Georgia started to wonder what the fuss was all about. "I just hate it when that happens," she remarked apologetically to the man beside her.

"I knew it would have to take a crisis before you'd grab my hand."

"Oh, I'm sorry." Her look was mortified. Her left arm was fully extended towards him, her hand locked in his. "Actually I had no idea I did that."

"If it makes you feel any better we could hold hands for the rest of the trip," he suggested.

"Forget it. My momentary panic is over," she confided though a thousand tingles prickled her skin.

He looked at her pale, slender hand for a moment before releasing it. "So there's nothing definite between you and Underwood?"

"I've asked absolutely nothing about *your* love life." Georgia gave him a severe look.

"What can I tell you? I'm not married."

"You're waiting for the right woman?"

"I've had to grapple with the possibility there mightn't *be* one."

"Well, you could present a formidable prospect to some. Not every woman can deal with corporate dynamos," she pointed out.

"It's pretty clear to *me* where your antagonisms spring from."

"It's a mistake to confide."

"And you do it so charmingly. Do you live alone?"

"I'm not in any relationship, if that's what you mean."

"I wondered about Underwood, that's all."

"You're *very* curious," Georgia returned.

"Not normally. But I haven't met anyone like you before."

"You must have." Her voice was laced with astonishment, a certain alarm.

"I'm sure I'd recall. Aside from all that, we're going to the same place. We're bound to run into each other."

Georgia didn't even try to keep the asperity out of her voice. "I admit it's a problem, but I'm there to relax, not for the social activities."

"My plans exactly." He settled his raven head and shut his eyes.

Georgia returned to her book, turning the pages for a full twenty minutes without taking in a word. Link Robards wasn't going to Sunset for nothing. His trip wasn't as simple or as innocent as that. There were a few possibilities. One was the Robardses were out to collect yet another hotel.

CHAPTER TWO

STANDING on her balustraded balcony, Georgia looked out over the dazzling tropical gardens to the fabulous crystal purity of the deep blue lagoon. Sunset was a glorious world. A world of seascapes and tropical flowers and plants. Towering coconut palms stood like sentinels in the grounds, at their feet beds of hibiscus of every known colour, with flowers of incredible size. There were countless other tropical plants, as well, flowers, shrubs, climbing vines all thriving prolifically in the year-round warm conditions. Everywhere Georgia looked she saw oleanders, frangipani, white ginger blossom, banks of gardenias, showy orchids and colourful bromeliads. In the shade of the water gardens grew wonderful ferns and aquatic plants. Dee had been acknowledged a great gardener. The grounds of Sunset were her living memorial.

Georgia hadn't spoken to her uncle as yet. He'd been busy when she'd arrived. They'd only exchanged a brief wave, but she expected he would pop in on her when he had an available minute. Though the grounds were as spectacular as ever, Georgia couldn't help noticing the hotel foyer badly needed refurbishing. There was a faintly scuffed look about the place. Even the furnishings in her room had seen better days. She would have to find out the full extent of her uncle's apparent plight. Perhaps she could help in some way. Georgia Bennett

Interiors had been doing rather well of late. She knew perfectly well how she could transform the foyer, indeed the entire entrance, but it would take money. Her father had plenty of that. The sad part was he and Uncle Robert had never really got on, and Dee had been a great one for taking the mickey out of Dawson Bennett.

Georgia took another deep breath of perfumed air then turned to her room. There was a magnificent basket of tropical fruits on the sideboard and another of white orchids like a flight of butterflies on the coffee table. The warm temperature and the sea breezes were just perfect. She felt better already, full of energy. She hoped as a matter of pride her uncle had alloted Link Robards one of the best rooms. Possibly he had taken one of the six self-contained villas that gave directly onto the beach via the gardens and white coral paths. Her uncle had offered her one, but as she was coming as his guest she didn't feel happy about commandeering the hotel's best accommodation. A room in the main building would do her fine.

Georgia was hanging up her chic resort clothes when there was a knock on her door.

She flew to it, her face wreathed in smiles. "Uncle Robert. How lovely to see you."

"Georgie girl!" He, too, was smiling broadly, using his and Dee's pet name for her. "There's no one, but *no one* like you. You look absolutely enchanting."

"I promise you I was quite ill." She smiled.

"It doesn't show, dear. I'm sorry I couldn't be there to greet you. I wanted to but I had a VIP arriving."

"It wouldn't be someone called Link Robards?"

"Now how did you discover that?" He swivelled in her direction.

"Simple. I met him on the plane. In fact we struck up some kind of rapport when we were both rushing for the taxi."

"I see," he said with a slight head shake. "I think he's looking the place over. In fact, I'm sure of it."

"That was my guess, too. But it's not on the market is it, Uncle Robert?"

For answer her uncle sighed deeply, then went to one of the floral upholstered rattan chairs and slumped into it, his handsome, weathered face tired and worn. "I'd be lying if I told you it's been easy going, Georgie. Sunset used to be my life, but it all means nothing without Dee."

"I know." Georgia sat on the matching lounge near him. "I feel for you, Uncle Robert, with all my heart. Dee was a wonderful woman. I know how much you meant to each other. It's only natural her loss has left an unfillable gap in your life. My life, too."

"And no children." Robert Mowbray whipped out a handkerchief and polished his glasses. "There *was* a time we were going to adopt. But then we bought the island, and the hotel became our child. It's sad, really. Only family matters. The great blessing was we had you, Georgie. Our godchild. How is my poor sister?" He slipped his glasses on his nose.

"It's hard to know with Mum. She always says she's fine."

"She could have had a much better life if she hadn't married Dawson," Robert murmured with some anguish. "She was such a *lovely* girl. Bright, too. None of us ever understood how she fell in love with such a domineering, difficult man. It's to your great credit, Georgie, you've shown him your mettle. You can stand on your own two feet. How's that barrister fellow, Underwood?''

She gave him a wry smile. "Fear no more. We've split up.''

"I can't say I'm not pleased. So full of himself for a young man, and that courtroom voice. I always felt I had to explain myself. There's something I'd like you to do for me tonight if you wouldn't mind.''

Robert Mowbray regarded his niece with a loving, grateful expression. "I've invited Link to have dinner with us. Myself and my niece. I thought it would be a nice gesture. I've met Link on a number of occasions. Conventions and the like. He's a very impressive young man. A brilliant architect, with all of his father's business acumen and drive. Sam had a major heart attack some years back. Someone told me he'd actually died, but there were paramedics on hand to resuscitate him. Big, handsome bloke, too. A bit of a rough diamond in the old days. He married Katherine Lincoln, a beautiful creature. To the manor born. Link got all the mother's class. Anyway you'd know that already. Would you help me out?''

"No problem,'' Georgia said, though her heart did a flip. "It might be a bit tricky. I didn't mention our connection.''

"Any particular reason why not?'' Her uncle peered at her.

"I wanted to remain incognito for a while. It struck me although he said he was here on holiday it could be business, as well.''

"It would be unusual for them to want to do up an old hotel," Robert Mowbray said.

"Sunset is very beautiful, Uncle Robert. And it does have an extensive fringing reef. The coral gardens are marvellous."

"There's that," he agreed. "They haven't moved into the north, as yet. On the other hand it could be just as Link said. He wants privacy. A quiet time with no one to bother him. He looks a very athletic chap. I expect he wants to sail, go scuba diving and the like. He's not married, either, in case you're interested."

"Now don't you start matchmaking," Georgia said. "You know better than anyone I don't go for the corporate dynamo type."

Her uncle looked at her for a few searching moments. "You sound like you're confusing him with someone like your father."

"The power brokers *do* have special qualities," Georgia pointed out with a wry smile.

"You must be looking at him differently. I find him charming. Courteous, too, which isn't always the case with the young lions. Anyway, I seem to remember he has some involvement with that Harper girl."

"Tania Harper?" Georgia experienced a rush of upset.

"She's the one who gets into all the social pages? Public relations director with one of Sam's hotels? Very glamorous creature with lots of dark hair."

"I swear she's had it bonded like Diana Ross. He never mentioned a girlfriend."

Her uncle shrugged. "Then it can't be a big deal. A

young man like that would have women swooning in a queue.''

"I'm afraid so," Georgia responded a little tartly, "but he's definitely not *my* type.''

"That's what Dee said about *me*. But we were blissfully happy for over thirty years.'' Robert Mowbray stood up, very tall and spare with thinning fair hair. "Now I must away, Georgie. I've got a number of things left to do. I want you to enjoy yourself while you're here. I don't want you paying for anything. You're here as my guest. Please remember that.''

"That's very generous of you, Uncle Robert,'' Georgia said gently. "But there must be something I can do for you in return. Some area where my professional expertise might come in handy.''

Her uncle hesitated for a moment. "The place *could* do with refurbishing. With guests moving in and out so frequently, things can become dilapidated very quickly. Dee used to attend to all that, as you know. I have to go now, but we'll speak of this again. Don't think I'm not proud of my clever niece. We may be able to work something out together.''

"What time this evening?'' Georgia asked.

Her uncle turned. "Would around seven suit you? We could have a pre-dinner drink in the lounge, then dinner in the Hibiscus Room. It's our best restaurant. Mario's promised to come up with something really special. It might make it easier if I simply introduced you as strangers.''

"That's okay. I don't want him to think we've discussed him, anyway.''

"Until this evening then.''

"I'm looking forward to it," Georgia said with an unusual mix of excitement and trepidation. Some people, she realised, had the power to change lives. Link Robards was one of them. Of that she was totally sure.

She couldn't resist a late afternoon swim in the lagoon. She gloried in the crystal water and its fresh, exhilarating effect. For more than an hour she gave herself up to the sea's seduction. The collage of colours was marvellous. Beyond the exposed pinnacles of the reef, the sea was cobalt, the lagoon a lambent turquoise fading into a lovely aquamarine then apple green before it ran up onto the pure white beach that girdled the small crescent-shaped emerald island.

The Great Barrier Reef was a wonderland, but as breathtaking as were the seascapes Georgia couldn't wait to explore the coral gardens, a fantastic kaleidoscope of colours and intricate designs and home to brilliantly patterned fish and aquatic creatures of astounding variety and numbers. The waters of the reef teemed with life. She supposed the dynamo would organise some big game fishing for himself while he was here. She wanted to see the Outer Reef if she possibly could. The Outer Reef bore the full brunt of the mighty Pacific's waves, the seaward side pitching steeply into the dark depths of the ocean. The only thing was it was difficult to see. Conditions had to be just right.

She, Uncle Robert and Dee had walked it once when she was around twelve. She had never forgotten the incredible experience or the fear that the tides would suddenly overtake them and they would be stranded in the middle of the ocean. One could walk for miles along the exposed reef, but very few people were foolhardy enough to wander too far. She remembered how the French navigator Bougainville had been so perturbed by the sight of the thundering, foaming breakers crashing against the mighty submerged rampart he had sailed away from the unknown continent to the islands of the South Pacific. It was Captain James Cook flying the British flag who had finally managed to navigate the perilous waters of the Great Barrier Reef. Once inside he must have thought he was this side of Paradise. It was an incredibly beautiful part of the world.

When Georgia finally came out of the water, the sun was sinking in a ball of fiery rose gold. Sunset was a magical time, the sky a glory, the last golden rays caught in the great feathery crowns of the palms. Lightly she towelled her body, already drying in the soft, warm breezes. She would have to wash the salt water out of her hair, but that was no problem. For now she caught it into a Grecian knot, then as she walked up the sandy slope she broke off a beautiful deep pink hibiscus and stuck it into her coil of hair. It was almost the deep fuchsia pink of her clinging one-piece swimsuit. She had a few bikinis, as well, but she always liked the classic one-piece for real swimming. Her skin all over was the colour of cream, but in a day or two it would turn the palest gold. She never sunbathed in full sun, but she always managed to pick up a perfect light tan.

Through the thick screen of flowering shrubs and golden canes she could see the South Sea style villas. It occurred to her she would like to reinvent them in a way that created much more of a sense of mystery and magic. So many ideas were already formulating in her head. She was very good with colour. That was one of her great strengths. An established Sydney firm had handled the last lot of renovations some years before. Even as a student Georgia had found the treatment much too safe for such a glorious environment, where nature's colours glowed like jewels. It had to be said, though, they had to please Dee, who had leaned more towards the practical than creating brilliant and imaginative effects. But it was an island, after all. The colours could be as dazzling as the colours of the world around them. She had the perfect suggestion for the foyer, a giant cupola to flood the interior with light, perhaps a beautiful fountain and a water garden beneath, but it would put her uncle to too much expense.

Transforming environments from drab to successful always made Georgia happy. Even a different palette of colours would make an enormous difference. *Solid* colours, not the almost washed out patterns that really hadn't survived the test of time. What she saw were all the brilliant colours of sea and sky, the whole spectrum of blues, greens, violets, the hot pinks of the bougainvillea and lots of white to reflect the purity of the white sands.

The prints on the walls needed changing, as well. She knew a wonderful young Queensland artist, one of her favourites, who specialised in painting the brilliant flora and bird life of tropical North Queensland, enchanting work, a blend of realism with fantasy. Now was the time to commission him before his work became too pricey. Georgia was so engrossed in her thoughts she didn't see the tall, broad-shouldered, lean-hipped athlete loping down the coral path towards her until it was too late.

"So what is someone supposed to do around here?"

Link Robards asked in that spiked yet so intimate voice. "Shout ahoy?"

She had been acutely aware of him on the mainland, but on the island his effect on her was nothing short of explosive.

"Surely you were walking into *me*?" Georgia pulled away almost violently, her sun-flushed body filled with a hot, peppery excitement. Even her skin felt singed where he'd touched her.

"As a matter of fact I did know you were on the beach," he admitted, silvery eyes cool as crystal. "I've been watching you sporting like a mermaid for the best part of an hour. Tell me, is it true you can breathe underwater?"

"Absolutely. For several seconds at a time." Considering how he was looking at her, Georgia was surprised how calm she sounded.

"From my vantage point it looked more like whole minutes." He towered over her, darkly, vividly handsome in white cotton trousers and a red and white striped casual shirt. "You look incredibly sensuous in that get-up."

"Tormentor." Her velvet soft eyes flashed. Sparks were flying wildly. In a moment she'd catch fire.

"I couldn't be more serious," he assured her. "I expect you know the hibiscus is the same colour as your swimsuit?"

"Actually it's a shade lighter." Georgia touched a hand to the large, brilliant flower, still in place.

"A tiny point, Miss Georgia. Dare I invite you to have dinner with me one evening? Tonight's on my mind, but I'm afraid I'm tied up."

"Really? And you've only just arrived. How did you manage that?"

"Duty, if you like. A courtesy. I know the owner. He's a very nice man and a bit of a matchmaker, I suspect. He wants me to meet his niece."

"She could be gorgeous!" Georgia offered sweetly, determined to look just that.

"Or she could be ever so *ordinary*. Either way I don't have the time for romance."

"How so?" Georgia moved out of a slanting ray of sunlight into the exquisite green cool. "Surely you're often mentioned with Tania Harper? Not that that's much to go on."

His sparkling eyes narrowed. "You surprise me, mermaid. You really do. You denied any knowledge of me."

"Quite true. It's only subsequently I've put two and two together."

"They still don't make five," he answered bluntly. "I was totally uncommitted up to a day ago."

"So, has someone new come into your life?"

"She appears to be working on it," he said in a challenging voice.

Every line of Georgia's fine, slender body registered confusion. "I beg your pardon?"

"How do you know I meant *you*?"

He laughed. She could see he was laughing at her. "It can't be *me*," she protested. "I can't *stand* men like you. Now if you don't mind, Mr. Robards, I'd like to get past."

He moved instantly, sunlight gilding his tawny skin. "The path *is* rather narrow. Romantic, too, if one cares for that sort of thing. Mercifully we don't. I only planned a stroll before dinner. Not an assignation. The sunset is quite glorious in this part of the world."

Georgia nodded, shouldering into her matching cover-up. *Too late.* "Can I ask you something?" She turned and looked at him. Odd little ripples were moving down her spine. And no denying them, either.

"Go right ahead." There was a trace of mild sarcasm.

"Why are you *really* here?"

His mouth firmed, and he raised his handsome head. "I take it you don't believe a *holiday*?"

"As a matter of fact, I don't."

He reached out abruptly and plucked the hibiscus out of her hair. "So what has it got to do with you?" The silver eyes were studying her very intently, brilliant against dark hair and skin.

"Nothing, really. I'm only using my intuition on this. You might as well tell me."

"I'm sorry, Georgia," he drawled. "I don't know you nearly so well."

He smiled just like a tiger, she thought.

"Well, it was worth a try." She gave him a little mocking finger wave. "Enjoy your stroll."

"May I call you?"

Georgia walked a few paces up the sandy slope before she turned. "I don't know yet. What would you want to say to me?"

"Hello, Georgia. That sort of thing."

"Then I guess that isn't a problem. I'm like you. The last thing I have on my mind is romance."

"Because of the big affair with Underwood?" He tilted an eyebrow.

"That could have something to do with it. And it wasn't any big affair, either," she added hotly. "So you don't have to sound so nasty."

"Nasty! My dear Miss Bennett, how extraordinarily touchy you are. On the whole you *do* need a holiday. It might make sense if we stuck together. Mutual protection and so forth. I couldn't help overhearing Underwood mention he'd see you soon."

"I'll figure out a way to stop him." Georgia tilted her chin. "Anyway, you may change your mind about sticking together when you meet the owner's niece."

The silvery eyes flicked over her. "I don't think so, Georgia," he said in a voice that made every bone in her body melt. "Ciao for now." He moved off, whistling melodiously that hit song of the Seekers from so many years before. It followed Georgia all the way from the beach.

She spent more time than usual dressing for dinner, in the end choosing a silk georgette toga-style dress that was like a caress on the body. The moulded ankle-length skirt split to show her legs. With it she wore gold sandals that laced up the leg on a classic Roman design. The colour of the dress was especially beautiful, neither blue nor violet but somewhere in between. She experimented with several hairstyles, looking to continue the theme, but finally decided on her usual straight shining fall.

She was going to a lot of trouble to make an impression on a man she knew could only endanger her, but there it was. Memories of those minutes on the coral path flooded her, the golden heat, the air full of sparks, the powerful effect he had on her. She had to face up to the fact she attracted him much as he made an ironic joke of it. These things did happen. The great thing was to be aware of it and take the appropriate defensive measures. Or so she told herself, applying a touch of heavenly fragrance.

As she entered the lounge every male head in the place shot up except the head of Link Robards, who had his back to her. Georgia threaded her way gracefully between the chairs, smiling at her uncle, who sprang to his feet, his face alight with love and pride.

"Georgia!" he called.

If he hadn't guessed beforehand, he certainly knew now. Georgia watched Link Robards rise to his impressive six three, turning courteously at her approach. For a spit second he let his true feelings show, then his dynamic face resumed its cool, practised charm.

"Georgia, darling!" Robert Mowbray kissed the smooth, flawless cheek Georgia presented. "You look lovelier than ever. May I present a young man who's behind the very best the hotel industry can offer. Link Robards. My niece, Georgia Bennett, Link. She runs her own interior design firm."

"How very clever and enterprising of you, Miss Bennett." Suavely Link Robards took Georgia's hand, applying just a little more pressure than was warranted.

So that was how he was going to play it. "I don't think I could possibly match *you*, Mr. Robards." Georgia gave him an admiring smile that didn't fool him one bit.

"Link, please," he insisted. "My name is actually James, but my mother called me Link right from the beginning. She was Katherine Lincoln."

"Why, thank you for sharing that with us, Link."

Georgia sat in the chair her uncle held for her. "And what do you actually *do* in the hotel industry?"

For an instant her uncle looked perplexed. Both Georgia and Link Robards were smiling, but there was a trace of something like smoke in the air. "Link is right-hand man to his father, Sam Robards, Georgie," he explained, trying to catch her eye. "I don't need to tell you who Sam Robards is, I'm sure."

"Oh, *sorry*!" Georgia touched Link's cream-jacketed arm impulsively. "The hotel tycoon, of course. I think that's marvellous."

He glanced at her with a don't-play-dumb-with-me expression. "It is as a matter of fact."

"Georgie, what would you like to drink?" her uncle intervened hastily, unsure just exactly what was going on.

"A glass of champagne would do nicely."

"You have something to celebrate?" Link Robards asked as his host turned away to attract the attention of the waiter.

"Catching *you* on the wrong foot. If only for a moment."

"I shouldn't be surprised." He sounded like it was obvious she had emotional problems.

"But you *were*?"

"I might do the same to you some time," he said with soft menace.

"We're getting a steady flow of guests into the lounge," Robert Mowbray remarked with satisfaction, turning to them. "Things were a little slow last month."

"You should put your niece's photograph on all your brochures," Link Robards suggested.

"She'd be perfect," Robert Mowbray agreed happily. "And she's so passionate about water sports." He immediately launched into a story about Georgia's brilliant sporting career since pre-kindergarten days. "Why, she could swim when she was barely two."

"Neptune's daughter. She's even wearing her goddess dress."

"You like it?" Georgia met the glittering diamond-hard eyes.

"Miss Bennett, your beauty takes my breath away."

A fraught fifteen minutes later they went in to dinner. Robert Mowbray was called away temporarily almost as soon as they'd ordered.

"You're annoyed with me, I suppose?" Georgia flashed a look at the striking dark profile. Already he'd picked up extra colour.

"Come on," he said crisply, "why wouldn't I be?"

"It was a harmless enough—"

"Deception?" he cut her off.

"I was going to say *charade*."

"To get me to talk?"

"About what?"

"Don't play the pansy-eyed innocent. I'm not impressed."

"Then that's a shame. I could have mentioned the connection, but the moment passed."

"At least you were right about the *gorgeous*," he taunted her. "Tell me, did you get yourself up tonight with me in mind?"

"Whatever do you mean?" She gave him a regal stare.

"That dress doesn't leave any possible doubt what

shape you're in." He studied her dryly. "If it's at all possible, it's a damned sight more seductive than the swimsuit."

"I'm always trying to look my best," Georgia said calmly.

"So I've got lots more to look forward to?"

"You're not worried, are you?"

"I'm enjoying it, as a matter of fact. As long as we can keep our relationship fairly casual."

"*What* relationship?" Despite herself her voice rose.

"Well, fate has rather shoved us together. Tell me, were you trying to get some information out of me to pass on to your uncle?"

"Mr. Robards, in this business, it's each man for himself."

His mouth twisted in a sardonic smile. "Really? You didn't seem so hard-headed to me."

"While you're the corporate dynamo," she retaliated. "That's largely why I'm so hostile towards you."

"There, now," he said maddeningly. "Your father must have given you a rough time."

"In many ways, I regret to say yes."

"But you've survived."

"Not only that, I've made my way. All on my own."

"Do I detect yet another challenge?"

She glanced quickly at him then away again. That blazing dark vitality. It made her feel almost giddy. "A simple statement of fact."

"Are you sure?" His voice had that abrasive quality again. "You've been dashing yourself against me ever since we met."

"So we've agreed I have a problem." Her heart

seemed to be thudding. "I wonder what's keeping Uncle Robert?" She sounded almost plaintive.

"I realise you're nervous."

"I am not!"

"Then what are those tiny little tremors in your fingers?"

Of course he was aware of her tension. "I think it has something to do with the way you're looking at me."

"Georgia, you're a woman men look at," he explained patiently. "Long blonde hair. Big brown eyes. Flawless skin. You'd stop conversations even without the beautiful feminine body."

"Be that as it may, no one else makes me want to turn and run."

"So what was it I witnessed at the airport?"

"I *told* you, Gavin and I are no longer an item," she said with a touch of heat.

"That's good, because you're better off without him," he said bluntly.

"You think so? And you've only seen him once."

"On the contrary. I was in court when he got that con man Jack Ullman off. I was a prosecution witness."

"When was this?" Georgia turned a perturbed face to him.

"I take it you don't know about it?"

"I vaguely remember the case. Gavin was thrilled about the outcome."

"He must have half the Mob calling on him." Contempt crossed his face.

Georgia paled a little. "Are you telling me it was a wrong decision?"

"It all came down to how the evidence was gathered.

Ullman was as guilty as hell. He got off on a technicality. All his victims knew that. A few days later one of them committed suicide. Ullman took his money and sent him to the wall.''

"I'm so sorry.'' Georgia swallowed, somewhat daunted by his demeanour. "But Gavin was only doing his job.''

"He used the law to get a guilty man off.''

"We all know it happens from time to time. I can't do much about it. It's an imperfect world. Gavin's a defence lawyer. I wouldn't care to defend someone I thought guilty myself, but someone has to do it.''

"I realise that, but I wouldn't have found a verdict like that something to rejoice over.''

"I suppose not.'' Georgia dropped her eyes. "Anyway, I've learned a few truths of my own about Gavin. He's in the past.''

"I don't think he intends to stay there.'' His look was both level and deep.

"If he wants to hold on to his career, he will. I don't intend to be harassed.''

"Good for you.'' The words were terse, holding a remembered anger.

A few moments later Robert Mowbray returned, apologising for his absence. "One of our more difficult guests,'' he explained. "The little boy was missing.''

"Missing?'' Georgia was dismayed. "You found him, didn't you?''

"Don't worry so, Georgie.'' Gently her uncle patted her hand. "The little scamp was hiding, that's all. I think myself as a way of gaining attention. The father is a very serious sort of chap. Very self-engrossed. He's

quite well known in the musical world, I believe. A pianist and composer."

"Not Adam Caswell?" Link asked quietly.

Robert Mowbray blinked behind his glasses. "I suppose I should keep it confidential, but seeing it's *you*,
Link, yes. No sign of a wife. Father and son are here by
themselves."

"How old's the little boy?" Georgia searched her uncle's face.

"Around six or seven. A problematic little fellow, I
would think."

"Probably he has reason to be," Link Robards remarked. "It's no secret the marriage isn't working. A
child would take that very hard."

"Poor little boy." Georgia's voice was sad. "It's
funny—" she began then abruptly stopped.

"What's funny?" Link Robards followed it up, his
look long and thoughtful.

"Oh, nothing. Better leave it."

"It sounded as though it might be important."

"How would you know that?" She was really starting
to feel he knew her too well.

"I've been studying you very carefully."

"What, exactly? The emotional content of my conversation?"

"Among other things." He smiled.

Its effect on her was like being on a roller-coaster,
and she hadn't been on one for years. Even the arrival
of the first course came as a very necessary breathing
space. Georgia had decided on the wonderful reef oysters steamed with ginger, shallot and chilli, and both men
chose entrees of roasted reef fish with a Thai sauce.

Georgia saw to her satisfaction the food was beautifully presented and tasted even better. Whatever else needed changing, it wasn't the chef, she thought thankfully.

All in all, it was a remarkably pleasant evening. They all settled on various seafood dishes for the main course. In such a part of the world it was impossible to go past the marvellous bounty of the sea. Mindful of her figure, Georgia delicately waved away any notion of dessert, but like most men her uncle and Link Robards had a sweet tooth, and made their selections from the delectable pastries on the trolley. Not that either of them carried a superfluous ounce for it, she thought with a twinge of envy.

The conversation ranged over a number of subjects, interesting and pleasant, nothing too profound. At no time was the possible fate of the hotel mentioned. Nor did Link Robards elaborate on his reasons for being there. Afterwards Robert Mowbray excused himself, and Georgia and Link were left together in the foyer.

"It's early yet," he said. "Would you like to go on to the nightclub?"

"Why not?" How easily rash decisions were made.

Inside the Hideaway a slightly passé chanteuse was singing the blues, an old Peggy Lee number. Her voice was very deep and throaty, and she was almost swallowing the mike.

"What do you make of that?" Georgia asked, sliding into an empty banquette.

"Marginally better than the bagpipes?"

"That's a little unkind." She looked at him, brown eyes reproachful.

"You started it. Now, what are you having to drink?"

"Mineral water with a twist of lemon."

"You certainly do things in style."

"I had two glasses of wine with dinner. That's all I allow myself."

"What a boon you are to society."

"*I* think so. There ought to be more like me."

"Modesty, Miss Bennett."

"I'm that, too."

"And so young to be so successful."

"I'm doing well, but I've a long way to go."

"*Bobby* can't speak highly enough of you," he said like a provocateur.

"Have you been checking up on me?" Georgia demanded.

"I do it all the time."

"You actually spoke to Bobby St. George?" Her eyes were huge in her creamy face.

"I didn't go so far as that. My mother looked you up."

"What?" Georgia felt like pounding the table.

"There's no need to look so perturbed. It was all very flattering."

"And what exactly was it in aid of?" She searched his face angrily.

"It crossed my mind you might try talking your uncle into refurbishing the hotel. Georgia Bennett Interiors hoping to get the commission, of course."

"Uncle Robert wouldn't be doing me any real favours. I really do know what I'm about. What's it to you, anyway?"

"I really like your uncle. I can see what a depressed state he's in. I haven't the slightest doubt you're as talented as you're beautiful, but your uncle might be taking a big risk allowing a virtual unknown with little corporate experience to take on a big and complex commission."

"So it's all altruism, is it?"

"Quite a degree of it."

"With the Robards's interests hidden behind a smoke-screen?"

"I told you, I came here for a holiday. It's my nature to look around."

"I do recall your saying the place needed a major overhaul."

"Do you disagree?"

She looked at him resentfully. "Oh, darn, you know I don't. You're quite right about Uncle Robert's depression. He and my late aunt were a devoted couple. When one is heartbroken it's difficult to take note of the surroundings. Dee always took care of the day-to-day maintenance. Uncle Robert managed the financial side of things."

"Then you know the hotel's losing money?"

"One doesn't have to be a corporate dynamo to realise that," she said tartly. "Uncle Robert has lost heart."

"And I understand entirely. I care about *my* father. His heart attack was a major trauma. I can imagine how shocking sudden death can be."

Georgia bent her head, and her hair fell around her face in a shimmering blonde curtain. "Frankly I don't know how he's standing up to his loss at all. He and Dee did *everything* together. They had no children."

"They had the next best thing. They had you."

"The three of us were very close."

"I can see the love you have for each other." He reached out and tucked her long hair behind her ear. "*Hello*, Georgia."

"Hello, James."

"Don't you dare." His voice was faintly rough and incredibly sexy.

"James is a nice name. It's a bit too tame for you, though."

"Well, Georgia's just right for you. When we get to know each other better I hope you allow me to call you Georgie."

"I'm sure you'd only turn it into a joke."

"What wrong with a joke now and then?"

The singer finished her bracket of songs, and they both clapped politely. "Where the heck's the waiter?" Link asked.

"Maybe he got restless and went out for a swim."

"Well, if the mountain won't come to Mohammed I guess I'd better go to the bar." He stood up and looked at her, the vivid, mettlesome, stunning male. "Still with the mineral water?" he asked dryly.

"Absolutely. What does Tania do? Toss off a few rums?"

"As I recall she goes for concoctions. Things with little purple umbrellas and great chunks of fruit."

"How do you stand it?" Georgia cast her eyes heavenward.

"Tania Harper, I have to tell you, is hotly pursued."

"How come she hasn't landed you?"

"I've been a contented bachelor for years," he said, a diamond dazzle in his eyes.

"All that has to *change*, James. The years are going by, and the dynasty must be secured."

"Would you like me to consider you?" he asked brazenly.

She shook her head. "The *very* last thing in the world I need is a high-powered husband. But I would like that cold drink."

He flashed her another one of those heart-stopping smiles. "Comin' up, ma'am."

CHAPTER THREE

GEORGIA awoke to a wonderful sense of well-being, a tingling anticipation of what the day might bring. It was just after seven but already the light was dazzling, illuminating a huge, blue glazed pot of yellow marguerite daisies on her balcony. There were hundreds of radiant heads, and Georgia found the sight enchanting. Bird calls sounded all over the island, a carolling counterpoint to the eternal song of the sea. The birds' colours were exquisite amid all the green.

She turned on her back, luxuriating in the knowledge she was on Sunset and didn't have to fly out of bed for an early morning appointment somewhere across town. Felicity and Martyn, her two assistants, would hold the fort for her. She deserved this break even if she could only manage ten days. In some ways she realised she was a workaholic like her father, but she knew she would never possess his stop-at-nothing ruthlessness to achieve his ends. The shocking truth was Georgia both loved and loathed her father. Her biggest sense of outrage, of powerlessness was reserved for her mother. Her parents had stayed together all these years, but Georgia was of the strong opinion her mother should have packed up and left long ago. She had won her own independence at a price. Her mother was still a prisoner in a gilded cage, an ornament to take out and display on all the right social occasions, but forgotten for most of the time. It wasn't as though Dawson Bennett had been faithful, either. Georgia and her mother both knew of his many transitory affairs. But her father wanted no part of divorce. He was married to a beautiful, refined, wealthy wife who long ago had elected to sublimate her will to his. The only thing her mother *had* been adamant about was Georgia's right to love and be loved by her grandparents and uncle.

Even that hadn't been easy, because Dawson Bennett bitterly resented any attention being directed away from him. *He* was to be the centre of his family's world. But Georgia had always loved her uncle Robert. Dee had occasionally put their close relationship at risk by openly questioning Dawson Bennett's opinions and judgments, delivered as they were from a position of pre-eminence. Dawson Bennett hadn't liked it, always referring to Dee as a woman who had "too much to say for herself." As a consequence Georgia had been refused permission to see them for months at a time. At these times Dawson Bennett praised his wife, who had "known her place" from the very beginning of their marriage.

In her early teens, when Georgia began to truly grasp her beautiful mother's entrenched sense of worthlessness, she began to press her to take action to resist her father's very real domination. But her mother could see no solution to her problems. She had married for better or worse, she told Georgia. Privately, Georgia considered her mother's spirit had been broken.

As always when Georgia began to think of her parent's marriage her mood became depressed. She couldn't allow that to happen at the very start of her holiday. Her mother had chosen her path in life. Georgia was determined the same thing wasn't going to happen to her. She leapt out of bed, deciding on an early morning run before breakfast. Her body was much admired, but it hadn't been achieved without discipline—watching what she ate and a daily exercise program. She was by no means a fitness freak, but she really did miss her daily run if she didn't go for some reason. Uncle Robert hadn't been exaggerating when he'd told Link Robards about her sporting prowess. As a schoolgirl she had dominated pool and track at her excellent fitness-oriented girls' school. In fact her friends had nicknamed her Atlanta after the fleet-of-foot goddess and the fact her Christian name was Georgia.

Dressed in a pink tank top and matching shorts, pink and white joggers on her feet, her thick blonde hair braided, Georgia studied herself in the mirror. She looked pretty good. Ready, in fact, for a three-mile run. The last thing Link Robards had said to her was, "I'll call you in the morning." She wasn't about to sit around waiting. The terrible irony was she was tempted. Attraction was like a monster. It gobbled up all one's natural caution.

For an hour Georgia ran, the sea breeze at her heels. She took the trail that encircled the island, meeting up with several other joggers, passing them with a wave, all the while looking out at the sparkling blue sea and the dreaming coral cays. One day she intended to have a picnic on Tryon, an unhabited coral cay she had been visiting since age ten, when Uncle Robert and Dee had taken over Sunset. Tryon was located on the windward side of Sunset, but was in easy striking distance when the tides were right. Tryon carried a light covering of trees and palms in addition to succulents and grasses, so there was plenty of shelter, but no water. It had been the Treasure Island of her childhood, mainly because Uncle Robert and Dee had always planted some little surprise for her to find. Usually she had come to Sunset alone. Her father had visited only once or twice, making nonstop criticisms as though Uncle Robert and Dee were his employees. Her mother only had to mention she might accompany Georgia on a visit for Dawson Bennett to find some pressing reason she shouldn't. Her place was by his side, not gallivanting up north.

On her return run, when she was nearing the hotel, Georgia veered off towards the beach. She unlaced her joggers and ran down to the lagoon. She dearly would have liked to walk straight into the water, but as she wasn't wearing a swimsuit, she settled for splashing herself generously with salt water. She had worked up a healthy sweat, so the blood ran clearly beneath her translucent skin, causing it to glow. The effect of the cold water was wonderfully bracing, and she continued to splash it over her face and throat so it ran down the upper slopes of her breasts and into the cleft. Her light sports bra and tank top were getting soaked. Had it been Tryon, with only the seagulls and noddy terns for company, she could have stripped off her clothes, but as it was her swim would have to wait. With a single quick motion she freed her braid, and her hair was caught by the wind and sprayed out all around her in long skeins of silk.

"Neptune's daughter!" someone called.

She recognized the voice. Smooth, assured, damn near hypnotic.

Link Robards.

Georgia turned, her heart kicking in like a motor. This man was something else! He was moving lithely over the sand, a tall and powerful figure in a swimsuit of dark tartan. Irresistibly he evoked a piece of sculpture, something heroic cast in bronze, broad-shouldered, deep-chested, tapering to the long, clean, narrow lines of the athlete. Everything about him turned her inside out.

"I'd thought of catching up to you on your run," he said as he drew closer, "but I didn't want to break your concentration." His sparkling glance held her in place while he studied her face, then the near drenched shirt that outlined so clearly the curves of her breasts. It was as if he knew how her flesh felt, its smoothness and texture. She needed to spin veils to protect herself.

"As a matter of fact I think you'd find it difficult to keep up with me," she retorted. "How did you know I went for a run, anyway?"

"I was up fairly early myself. Had a swim, did a bit of exploring and there you were! Running like a gazelle up the trail. Why didn't you wear a swimsuit?"

And have you send what's left of my composure up in flames? Ah, no!

Georgia turned her gaze to the lagoon and managed to sound casual. "I was thinking that myself."

"So what have you planned for us today?"

He hadn't moved an inch, yet she felt she had lost her own body space. The two of them might just as well have been enclosed in a giant bubble.

"I haven't planned anything." She shrugged, momentarily nonplussed.

"I thought we agreed it would be best to stick together."

"I said nothing of the kind."

"You can't talk your way out of it, Georgia," he teased. "Besides, there are endless possibilities. What about scuba diving off the reef?"

"Do you usually get what you want?"

His brief laugh held the suggestion of irony. "Like you, I've been spoiled."

"I don't know that *I've* been spoiled," she said, thinking of her dysfunctional childhood.

"I'm ready to listen." Very gently he reached out and pushed a long strand of hair behind her ear. In the process his hand brushed her cheek.

"Actually I don't need anyone to straighten me out." She swallowed against the sudden rush of sensations.

"Talking about it might help. It's odd how we keep the most important things about ourselves secret."

She turned her head away. "Link, I don't know you. I don't know that I trust you, either."

"When I'm more trustworthy than most. Your friend Gavin, for one," he said bluntly.

"Let's leave Gavin out of it." Her voice picked up heat.

"I don't think he's going to give you the chance. That's only *my* opinion, of course. You know him so much better."

"I find it extraordinary you should be concerned."

"Actually it's taken *me* by surprise, as well. I think it has something to do with the fawn's eyes. Behind the softness there's *hurt*."

"You see that, do you?"

"Very clearly." Something in his smile wrung her heart. Lord, did she show it so badly? Her emotional deprivation?

"So are we going diving or not?"

She could have drawn back. There was time. Instead she found herself saying, "Why not? It'll give me an opportunity to show off."

Back in her room Georgia took a quick shower to cool down. Link Robards was having an incredible effect on her, a mixture of caution and excitement. She felt charged. Full of energy and passion, even when all the warning bells were going off.

On her way to breakfast her progress was arrested by a curious sight. The contents of a laundry basket standing outside one of the empty rooms were stirring and bunching as though they had come alive. Georgia had one panicky moment thinking of snakes, but of course there weren't any on the island. She stepped out valiantly, wondering if it could possibly be a pet that belonged to one of the staff. If so, it had no place playing near the guestrooms, much less hiding in a laundry basket.

She peered into the empty room, expecting to see a maid going about her business, but there was no one around. She turned back and picked up a long-handled duster standing against the wall. A few exploratory pokes should do it.

The cry that resulted took her by surprise. No bark, but a loud little-boy squeal. Georgia threw back the laundry, her astonished eyes meeting those of a child around six or seven. Beautiful sapphire blue eyes stared up at her from beneath a thick, dark, shining fringe sitting flush with his eyebrows. The classic "puddin' basin" cut.

"Well, really!" she said. "You nearly gave me a heart attack."

"I'm sorry." He grinned at her as though sharing a good joke.

"That's all right. All's forgiven. Do you need a hand getting out of there?"

"No way!" He sent the basket crashing to the floor, then rolled out.

"What were you doing, anyway?" Georgia helped him up.

"Just having a bit of fun. Dad's asleep and I'm bored."

"Well, you can't play in the laundry baskets."

"I won't anymore. I just got the idea when the cleaning lady moved off."

He was a very thin little fellow but undeniably cute, with a look of high intelligence that sat oddly on his narrow shoulders. He wasn't dressed for the beach, either. More like he was about to give a violin recital, right down to an incredible bow tie.

"So what's your name?" Georgia asked, curious and intrigued.

"Leon." He gave her a smile like a magic wand.

"How do you do, Leon, I'm Georgia." Georgia held out her hand, and the little boy shook it with considerable aplomb. "Leon's an unusual name. I like it."

"Mummy's idea. I was born in August. You know, Leo the lion?"

"I sure do." Georgia smiled. "I'm another one. Isn't that nice?"

"Yes. It makes us friends."

"Good, so we can talk. What room are you in, Leon? Are you with your parents?"

The little boy unexpectedly dropped his head. "Mummy doesn't live with us anymore."

"Oh, I'm sorry." Georgia's tender heart smote her. She patted the little boy gently on the shoulder.

"They're not getting divorced or anything," Leon told her hastily, his heart in his blue eyes. "It's a separation."

"I'm sure it will work out, Leon," Georgia said.

"Oh, so am I." He sighed deeply. "Mummy couldn't listen to Daddy playing the piano all the time."

Of course. Adam Caswell, Georgia thought. This must be his little boy.

"Sometimes he plays it *all night*." Leon gestured with upturned hands. "I never hear him, but Mummy says it drives her batty."

"Perhaps Daddy should think of a soundproof room," Georgia suggested.

"It's a really *big* house," Leon said with great loyalty. "Mummy doesn't love music like Daddy and I do."

"I see." Georgia shook her head a little helplessly. "So have you had your breakfast?" she asked more brightly by way of diversion.

"Nope, and I'm hungry."

"I'm not surprised." Georgia glanced at her watch. "It's past eight-thirty. I'm sure Daddy's up by now. I'll take you to your room." Georgia took his hand, and he didn't resist. Rather her presence seemed to offer com-

fort. Obviously he was badly missing his mother.
"Which is it?"

Leon pointed. "Twenty-four A. I'm B. Daddy is composing something now. It's all about the sea. That's why
we're here. Daddy's very clever. Grandpa says it's
Mummy who has the little problem."

They were almost at the room when a tall, very thin
man emerged, looking anxiously up and down the cor-
ridor. He was somewhere in his late thirties, good-
looking in a nerve ridden way, with long dark hair drawn
back into a ponytail and soulful dark eyes.

"Leon!" he called, relief mixed up with exasperation.

"It's okay, Dad," Leon answered cheerfully. "This
is Georgia. We met in the hallway."

"Hello, there, Mr. Caswell, Georgia Bennett,"
Georgia introduced herself as they met up. "I hope you
weren't worried?"

"Not really. Leon's very good at taking care of himself." He gave her his son's illuminating smile, a smile
that wiped the intensely retrospective look from his face.
"I do hope the little monkey wasn't bothering you."

"Not at all," she disclaimed. "We've had a pleasant
conversation, but now Leon's hungry."

"Of course!" Adam Caswell struck a hand to his forehead. "I'm afraid I slept in. I was working into the early
hours. Poor Leon. He doesn't have much of a father."

Immediately Leon went to his father and hugged him
around the knees. "That's all right, Dad. I told Georgia
you were composing something special."

"It's a great honour to have you on the island, Mr.
Caswell." Georgia smiled.

"Please, it's Adam." All the time he was talking,

Adam Caswell was studying Georgia intently, rather as one might study an inspirational figure. It was slightly disconcerting.

"You're very beautiful," he said at last.

"Thank you." Georgia accepted the compliment gracefully. "I can't take any credit. I have a beautiful mother. By the way it's my uncle who owns and runs this hotel, Robert Mowbray. Perhaps you didn't know, but we have an excellent child minding facility for when parents need a little time to themselves or the children want company of their own age. They're supervised at all times."

"That's handy to know."

"Well, I must be on my way." Georgia looked at Leon and smiled. "I'm sure we'll meet again."

"Can I come down to breakfast with you, Georgia?" Leon pleaded. "Dad will take ages."

"Leon, *please*. We can't impose on Miss Bennett any longer," his father hastily intervened.

Georgia considered briefly. She didn't really mind taking Leon to breakfast. "No imposition at all."

Adam Caswell's smile grew. "In that case, behave yourself, young man. It's very kind of you, Miss Bennett. Breakfast is not a meal I'm much interested in."

"And they say it's the most important meal of the day," she said lightly.

"That's what *Mummy* says, too," Leon piped up. "She says Dad would be all the better if he ate properly."

Adam Caswell smiled helplessly.

"Can we go out onto the terrace, Georgia?" Leon asked excitedly when they arrived in the dining room.

"Of course, but we'll get breakfast first. It's buffet style."

"Great!" Leon looked elated. "We've had meals in our room ever since we arrived."

"Then this morning we'll make up for it." Georgia led the child to the buffet, where a dozen or more guests were making the most of a wealth of dishes. "Would you like me to help or do you want to serve yourself? There's no need to pile the plate. We can keep coming back if you want a little more."

"You do it, Georgia. No cereal. I hate it."

"What about some fruit instead? The sliced mango looks nice."

"Oh, I don't mind mango." Leon sounded much relieved. "Then I want— "

"Sausages, bacon and hash browns."

He smiled, blue eyes alight. "And maybe an egg if you turn it upside down."

A short time later they were seated at their table on the sun-drenched terrace with its foaming balustrade of Thai pink bougainvillea. Georgia sipped at her grapefruit juice. Leon speared succulent slices of mango and popped them into his mouth.

"This is *much* better than muesli," he paused to say. "Why doesn't Mummy know about it?"

"I'm quite sure she does. Maybe you could alternate the fruit with the cereal. There are all kinds of cereals. The one with the Iron Man on the box is quite nice. Good for you, too. All the champion swimmers and Iron Men eat their cereal."

Leon nodded and took a sip of orange juice. "I don't really have to bother, Georgie, I'm going to be a musician like Dad."

"Really? You've made up your mind so early?" Georgia was impressed.

"I'm a prodigy, Georgie, didn't you know?" Somehow Georgia had turned into Georgie.

"I should have guessed." Georgia smiled. "You have that air about you. What instrument do you play?"

"The piano like Dad. Not his Steinway. He has a big concert grand. I have to make do with an upright until I'm older."

"So what does Mummy think about having a prodigy for a son?"

"Oh, she doesn't mind me," Leon said artlessly. "She's proud of *me*. So what do *you* do, Georgie?" he asked in his surprisingly adult fashion, smiling his thanks as Georgia removed his fruit bowl and set his cooked breakfast before him.

"I'm an interior designer. Do you know what that is?"

"Sure!" Leon hooted. "Mummy had an interior decorator do up the farmhouse where we lived. She said it was spooky the way it was. All the gloomy rooms! Dad and I *liked* it, but Mummy said being in the country was ruining her life."

Georgia was beginning to think Mummy and Daddy were like chalk and cheese. "It's not a working farm, Leon?" she asked, quite unable to see Adam Caswell on a tractor.

"Dad's the only one who works," Leon said. "Sometimes he even falls asleep at the piano. Grandpa said he should take a holiday before he has a breakdown. He and Mummy squabble all the time. I *hate* it when they're like that." He shook his head gloomily.

"I'm sorry, Leon." Georgia gripped a small hand for a moment, then deliberately changed the subject.

"I'm looking forward to hearing you play. I learned the piano myself. In fact, I sat all my exams and gained two diplomas while I was still at school."

"Did you go on to the conservatorium?" Leon asked and opened his mouth for more sausage.

"No, I went on to university. I'm not all that good, Leon. Certainly not a prodigy. But I love music."

"What would you like me to play for you?" Leon asked, buttering a slice of toast.

"I don't know your repertoire. It took a few years before anyone wanted to listen to me."

"Do you know Mozart's Sonata in C?" Leon asked.

"You can't play *that*! Surely?"

"I can, too."

"Then you're indeed a prodigy, Leon. I do envy you."

From music they moved on to sports, but Georgia was surprised to hear Leon couldn't swim when all the children she knew of Leon's age could. "We'll have to do something about that while you're here. That's if Daddy says yes."

"I'm sure it'll be O.K." Leon set down his knife and fork. "As long as Dad doesn't have to come. He's not the least bit interested in sports. Not even *cricket*." This with amazement.

"I could arrange a lesson this morning," Georgia said, after a brief consideration.

"With *you*, Georgie?" Leon asked hopefully.

"No. We have a professional coach. Bill Draper. He's great with kids. For that matter there are quite a few children on the island. Would you like to meet them?"

"Dad mightn't want me to get involved," Leon said uncertainly. "He's a very quiet person."

"But you have to have young companionship, Leon. Why don't you let me speak to him?"

"Gee, thanks, Georgie." The little boy brightened. "Why don't we ask him as soon as we're finished? I think I could just fit in that little Danish pastry."

"You've got a good appetite." Georgia smiled and passed the basket.

It took quite some time to get Leon settled, but Georgia didn't regret the demands on her limited time. Sunset was family-oriented, and children were well catered for. Leon would join the other children for his swimming lesson, and he seemed quite agreeable about joining the games that had been organized for the day. It hadn't taken her more than five minutes to gain Adam Caswell's approval, though Georgia couldn't remember a time when she'd met such a self-absorbed man. It was apparent he loved his son, indeed was very proud of him, but he lived for his music. Georgia wondered how he would survive without his beloved Steinway. There were pianos on the island and a baby grand in the Hideaway, which he was welcome to play if he cared to, but it seemed he had no need of any instrument to work out his compositions on manuscript. Had he been a more outgoing man she might have asked him something about the opus he was working on, but she didn't want to get too close. From the way he stared at her she had the feeling she might be landed with the role of muse.

Having offered to collect Leon after his swimming lesson, Georgia was surprised when Adam Caswell found his way to the pool, stopping to chat with her for several minutes before taking Leon off to dress. It was as she was walking to the main building that Georgia encountered Link, who was drinking coffee under one of the fringed umbrellas.

"Care to join me?" he asked, standing up and pulling out a chair. "I was looking for you, as a matter of fact, but your uncle told me you were busy organizing the Caswell boy's day."

"Someone had to do it," Georgia said, meeting those brilliant all-seeing eyes. "An iced coffee would be nice."

"Anything with it?" He signalled the waiter and gave the order.

"Good lord, no. I have to work off breakfast."

"Which you had with young Leon." He sat down again. "Didn't his father care to join you?"

"He wasn't asked."

"I did tell you the marriage is said to be on the rocks."

"Just a minute, now," Georgia warned.

"Let me finish. Then again it could be saved. Should be, for the boy's sake."

"You want to warn me about something?"

"Georgia, I couldn't help noticing the way Caswell was staring into your face."

"With all due modesty, I have to tell you I'm used to being stared at."

"Indeed, yes," he drawled. "After all, I've stared at you myself, but there was too much intensity about it, that's the trouble. He looked like a man who's been on some inspirational journey then found the answer right under his nose. Surely you got that feeling, as well?"

"Link, what are you talking about?" She sighed.

"It's not all that complicated. In fact, you *know*."

"It's the little boy who appeals to me. Not the father."

"Then I suggest you make that perfectly plain, Georgia, otherwise you might land yourself in an unwanted situation."

"Thanks for the advice," Georgia answered.

"I'm a kindly soul."

"Really? You sound more like you're on a crusade. Anyway, I thought we were going to use one another for mutual protection."

"It does hold the key to a trouble-free vacation, don't you think?" he asked tauntingly. "Ah, here's your iced coffee. What time would you like to head off this afternoon?"

"With the tide. We'll need to organise the gear. Fill the tanks."

"I've already seen to everything." He gave her that charming, mocking smile. "Tell me, just for the fun of it, how would you go about refurbishing the hotel if you had a chance?"

"What, little me, the virtual unknown?" Georgia raised her delicate eyebrows, reminding him of his words.

"Don't take it so much to heart. After all, you're only twenty-four or so."

"Would you care to check my teeth?"

"Dear me," he tutted. "I didn't call for a copy of your birth certificate. Your uncle happened to mention your age in passing. How much you've achieved in such a short time. Words to that effect."

"I see." She relaxed slightly. "Well, I have to tell you, Link Robards, I'm not going to allow you to pick my brains."

"So what do you charge for a consultation?"

"I have to *like* the client first."

"Which is why I asked. You *do* like me, Georgia. In fact, you want to have dinner with me tonight."

"I didn't come to Sunset to pick up strange men." she said coolly. "So what would *you* do to the hotel, you brilliant architect?"

"How about start again?" he answered bluntly.

"You mean *demolish* the place?" Georgia's dark eyes widened.

"It's a hypothetical case, of course. We're two professionals. We can discuss it objectively."

"Hypothetical? Is that so?" Georgia gave a brittle laugh. "If your name weren't Robards. If you and your father weren't perhaps thinking of investing in North Queensland. It's the top tourist destination in the country, after all. The Great Barrier Reef is one of the wonders of the world."

"Interestingly enough, I was sold on it long ago, Miss Bennett. In fact I might know this part of the world rather better than you."

"Well, you've got a good ten years' start," Georgia retaliated in a tart voice.

"For your information, Miss Bennett. I'm thirty-one," he countered.

"Which is regarded as almost middle-aged by many." She smiled sweetly.

"You mean like young Leon?"

Georgia's smile broadened at his perceptiveness. "He tells me he's a child prodigy."

He laughed. "Well, he certainly knows a beautiful woman when he sees one. And how to start up a friendship. What instrument does he play?"

"The piano."

"Then you'll have to arrange a little concert if he's agreeable. He looks a nice kid. Pity about the haircut."

"Lord, yes!" Georgia sighed. "His fringe is falling right into his eyes. I think I might ask permission to have his hair cut at the salon. And he needs some casual clothes."

"I thought you came for a holiday, not to play nanny." His tone had an odd inflection in it.

"But Leon's here, and he needs help."

His glance whipped over her and lingered on her full, soft mouth. "Bless your tender heart, Georgia, but why don't you leave it to his father? I don't think he's quite a clueless as he looks."

"Nerve-ridden," Georgia corrected. "I thought he looked nerve-ridden."

"Just the sort of people I've learned to avoid."

"Of course. You're the corporate dynamo, while he's a musician from a totally different world."

"What have you got against corporate dynamos when you're a dedicated career woman yourself?" he asked.

"Maybe I've got a few skeletons locked away in the cupboard."

"The answer to that is to open up the cupboard."

"I've considered that, but I don't think it would work." Briskly Georgia changed the subject. "So you'd pull down the hotel, would you?"

"Shh, Georgia." He put an elegant, tanned finger to his shapely mouth.

"You're very devious, Link Robards." Devious. Dangerous. Devastating, she thought, feeling as though her body was made of melting wax.

"It's not a mortal sin, is it? Anyway, I look seriously at all aspects of the hotel industry. Your uncle established this resort some fifteen years ago. He did a good job. But that was *then*. I think the whole concept should be changed."

"And which way would *you* go?" Georgia asked in a satiric voice, trying to steel herself against him.

"One central complex and individual bungalows all around the island," he said, enthusiasm in his voice. "Many of the other islands cater for families. They're bigger, less fragile. I see Sunset as a private retreat for adults only. People who care deeply about these small, very special sanctuaries."

"So you'd shut out the kids?" For a minute Georgia overreacted on principle.

"Listen," he said reasonably. "You know as well as anyone the damage inflicted on reefs by increasing numbers of tourists. Sunset has a very beautiful fringing reef. Your uncle told me himself he's become worried by the amount of damage inflicted on it of recent times. It can't be allowed to become substantial. Not everyone teaches their child to become environmentally sensitive. Coral boulders get overturned and delicate corals smashed in the hunt for all the shells. Children are the worst offenders when it comes to overcollecting. You've been coming here since you were a child. You must know some of the most beautiful specimens are no longer common. Even the walking track around the island is being overused. I would definitely cut numbers. No more than fifty guests at any one time. Change the concept, as I said.''

''And what about Uncle Robert? I'm sure you're aware he doesn't have that kind of money.''

''No.''

''So you're here to report to your father?''

''You sound as though you'd like to send me to prison,'' he observed rather tersely. ''I think you could describe this trip as a mixture of pleasure and business. I needed a short, quiet break and I wanted to see how one of the smaller resorts operates. There was no plan, Georgia. Only a looksee with a bit of paradise thrown in.''

''A very *keen* looksee,'' she commented, meeting the light piercing eyes.

''I'm sure you realise one has to be very keen to survive.''

She shrugged a shoulder. ''If it means anything at all, I agree with you about reducing numbers. I don't want to see the reef damaged any more than you, but we could keep the central complex as guest accommodation and build some more bungalows over a period of time.''

''The central complex already needs a great deal of money spent on it. The foyer is too dark.''

"I've been thinking about that. I'd go for a giant cupola. A beautiful big dome to let in the light. I'd put a fountain beneath it and a lush water garden."

"Would you, indeed?"

"Don't patronise me, Link Robards."

"Come on, was I doing that?"

"It's all in your regard. But to continue, I'd change the colour scheme, as well. Dee had a very practical bent, and one can understand why, but I'd mirror all the brilliant jewel colours of the island."

"And you're looking to your uncle to offer you the job?"

It was said smoothly, but Georgia stood up, hot colour glowing beneath her luminous skin. "I wasn't aware we had to get the okay off you."

"Don't be like that, Georgia. I only asked a question." He caught hold of her hand. Held it, while her heart fluttered like beating wings.

"Really? I thought you were spending a lot of time prying into our affairs."

"You were throwing a few smokescreens yourself. Now, we didn't actually set a time for our dive, did we?"

"I was waiting for you to *tell* me," she said shortly. "You're the dominant type."

"And here I was thinking I was just an ordinary guy."

A few people on the terrace were beginning to look their way, so Georgia swooped down close to him and murmured into his ear. "You're abrasive and you're jarring and I don't trust you at all. Two o'clock will do just fine."

''Splendid!'' He gave her that quirky, mocking smile and released her hand. ''Shall we say the jetty?''

''The jetty it is.'' She nodded to him briskly, though her flesh was all a-tingle. ''I hope you know how all your gear works. I just might leave you out there.''

CHAPTER FOUR

THOUSANDS of glorious little fish came to stare at them, mouths agape at these alien creatures in their exquisite realm. The water was so transparent Georgia could see from the hull of their fifteen-foot dinghy almost to the sea floor. The enormous clarity of her vision was further illuminated by the dazzling beams of sunlight that broke through the gaps in the reef and rayed deep into this silent green-lit world.

From time to time myriads of small silvery-blue fish covered with draperies like floating chiffon swum over her in shoals, dimming the light with their sheer numbers before darting into the multicoloured branching corals as delicate as fern gardens. The beautiful little butterfly fish were quite friendly, fluttering slowly and gracefully around her like the exotic butterflies in the rain forests of the mainland. Several feet away from her in the marvellous staghorn corals the Morish idols hovered, easily identifiable with their yellow, white and black stripes, playful companions to the harlequin fish with their bright bands of red. Georgia had learned long ago why so many of the coral reef fishes were so brilliantly marked and coloured. There were so many species of fish on the reef, characteristic colour patterns had evolved for inter-and intra-specific recognition. Males could be distinguished from females, and the fantastic range of colours in the corals provided very effective camouflage from predators.

The little seahorses Georgia loved floated in and out of the waving seagrasses, the axis of their bodies held vertically while they propelled themselves along with their small dorsal fins. Georgia found it extraordinary that many coral reef fish like the butterfly, damsel and angelfish adhered strictly to their own patch, selecting a specific coral clump and rarely straying from it for their life span. The larger fish moved farther afield in schools, but even they adhered to a particular reef.

A short distance from her Link was reaching out a hand to a curious butterfly fish, deep violet in colour with a multitude of trailing winglike fins. It was quite extraordinary how quickly the undersea creatures came to accept you if you didn't do anything to frighten them. As experienced divers she and Link were staying close together for mutual protection. They'd also agreed on exploring only one particular section of the reef for that day and then only for an agreed length of time. Both of them knew it was as easy to lose oneself in the coral jungles as it was to become disoriented in the mainland rain forests. The reef was the greatest known storehouse of corals, some three hundred species compared with the Caribbean's eighty.

In such an environment scuba diving was very popular, but one had to take sensible precautions. With waters of such crystal clarity it was difficult to correctly estimate water depth and as a consequence it was easy to dive too deeply. Then, too, the marine environment was so full of exquisite sights it was all too easy to lose track of time. Neither of them was getting too near the coral pinnacles. It was easy enough to get the scuba gear hooked.

Above them their dinghy was flying the international diver's flag, and they had taken care to gauge the strength of the currents before swimming away from it. Link wasn't wearing a wetsuit. Neither was she. They'd both agreed wetsuits became uncomfortably hot in the tropics. She wore a Lycra swim shirt over her bikini. Link wore an old shirt and shorts. At least it was some protection from coral lacerations should they be washed into it, but the currents were calm.

For Georgia and Link it was an enthralling experience exploring the deep water, a fantasy filled with the most beautiful aquatic wonders where giant flowers of all shapes and colours grew. Every kind of coral known to man was represented. Every conceivable colour. Pink, orange, scarlet, mauve, bright purple and vivid green. There were huge colonies of indigo blue mushroom corals fringed by circular fans of amethyst, carpets of soft yellow corals tipped with blue and green buds, ruby and almond-green organ pipe corals that were so aptly named. It was such an incredible world Georgia had the feeling it wasn't of this planet but the dream world of science fiction.

On the under surfaces of the coral boulders, in the crevices and caverns, a fantastic array of sponges occurred, not ordinary sponges like the ones used in the bath but all shapes and colours. The armoured crustaceans, too, showed an amazing variety of form and colour, some glowing like opals as they scurried into the dense petrified forest. One of the features of the Great Barrier Reef was its tremendous species richness.

Georgia knew this was because of its precise location in the tropics, lying as it did near the centre of the vast Indo-West Pacific region where marine life was the most prolific.

Time simply flies when you're one with the fishes, Georgia thought. She and Link were drifting together as a pair, rather in the manner of the glorious little butterfly fish who swam mostly in twos. It was less than a minute after Link pointed to his underwater watch, the signal that their time was up, that they had their only encounter with danger, though both knew from experience the sea could be as violent as it was beautiful. During their dive they had seen sea snakes, eels, stringrays, manrays, huge fish of all kinds. Now they were confronted by a twenty-foot tiger shark.

It materialized from behind a towering coral pinnacle, swimming directly towards them, an awesome sight because of its bulk and fearsome reputation. While it was true most sharks took no notice of divers intruding into their silent green domain, it was a heart-stopping moment. In a split second Georgia recalled tiger sharks had been involved in fatalities in Queensland waters but rarely in the Great Barrier Reef waters where there was an enormous abundance of natural prey. When the shark came within a couple of metres of them both clapped their hands, not an easy thing to do underwater, but the startled shark caught the sound. It turned a half circle in dazzling time, fleeing in the opposite direction but leaving the crystal waters churned up with white bubbles.

They made it to the boat in record time, heaving themselves over the side and disposing of their cumbersome scuba gear in a silence that was broken only by the sound of the gulls and their harsh breathing.

"You've a hell of a nerve," Link grunted finally, leaning over to help her remove her flippers and protective leg knife.

Now the danger was over she could afford to be flippant. "You didn't think I was just going to *freeze*?"

He looked at her hard, his manner unfathomable. Was he angry with her? Pleased with her? What? "I know you're an experienced diver," he said tersely, "but, lady, a tiger shark is one frightening sight."

"Trust me, I know." She smiled sweetly, squeezing sea water out of her thick golden plait. "Anyway, you know as well as I do sharks don't attack as a matter of course. They get more than enough to eat on the reef."

"This isn't funny!" he snapped.

"Hey, what's wrong?" She stared at him in perplexity. He looked too damned tall. Powerful. Magnetic. *Male*. His splendid body was a dark silhouette against the blazing blue sky.

He shrugged abruptly, obviously trying to lighten up. "I'm searching myself for the answer. I have to tell you I was infinitely more worried about you than me."

"But I didn't let you down, did I?"

"No." His eyes swept her. "In fact, congratulations are more in order." He lowered himself onto the bench beside her.

"So what do you have in mind?" She hadn't meant to be provocative. Not at all, only his eyes flared with intense brilliance.

"Only this." He caught her chin, turned her face to him, staring for a moment at her wet, parted mouth, with its slick, cushiony surface. "You really are Neptune's daughter," he murmured.

She felt so strangely weakened she couldn't move. His fingers slipped down her throat while his mouth came down over hers in one long, hard kiss that left all her senses flooded. She knew she was supposed to take the kiss as it was meant. A celebration of life. Recognition of a shared danger. But it told her more powerfully than anything else could have done that this man had the potential to change her life.

There was a message from her uncle when Georgia returned to her room, suggesting they might make a quick inspection of the hotel in the late afternoon. It sounded as though he was serious about carrying out refurbishments, Georgia thought, a decision he made clear when she found her way to his office.

"I've been in such a daze, Georgie," he confided, removing his glasses and rubbing his eyes. "I've let things slide. It's taken you and Link to shock me out of it." He put his glasses on.

"What has Link said?" Georgia looked startled.

"Nothing, but he has that all-seeing regard. I expect he finds the place pretty shabby after what he's used to."

"He understands your situation, Uncle Robert. I'll say that for him. His father's heart attack then bypass operation obviously caused him great concern. They must be close."

"So I've heard. Sam Robards has the reputation for being a mighty tough man. Came from nothing, married well. But I told you that. How did the diving go?"

"Wonderful!" she said casually, though it cost her an effort. "Even had an encounter with a tiger shark."

"Georgie!" Robert Mowbray looked dismayed and astonished.

"It wasn't a real problem, just a bit of a scare. The shark was more frightened of us than we were of it."

"It's as well our waters are teeming with fish. I couldn't bear to see our one-hundred-per-cent safety record broken. What do you think of Link?" Robert Mowbray looked at his niece over his glasses.

"To tell the truth—" Georgia picked up a paperweight and set it down again "—I'm attracted to him. Don't know that it's bright, but it's the way it is."

"And he's as attracted to you?"

"Perhaps. But it could never work out."

"Why not?"

"I know what it's like living with high-powered men."

Robert Mowbray sighed. "I blame your attitude on your father. He might be high-powered but he's also without humour and so domineering. I don't want to hurt you, Georgie, I know you want to love him, but he's ruined my sister's life. She doesn't even *have* one. You can't call running around art galleries living. Why, she's never crossed him. She won't even come up here for a visit if he says no."

"There's not much we can do about it," Georgia said. "Mum made her own bed, now she's got to lie in it. Not *my* words, hers. I have to admit I've suffered, as well. Dad always gave me everything I wanted. In the material sense. The only thing he tried to deny me was my independence."

"But you got it anyway."

"Not without many upsets and a lot of harsh words," Georgia said, struggling to keep her tone calm. "The thing that really upset me was Mum never took my part."

"She had problems. She was married too young," Robert Mowbray said flatly. "Dawson moulded her into just the sort of woman he wanted. Unswervingly loyal but with no mind of her own."

"Don't let's talk about it," Georgia begged. "It raises my blood pressure just as much as yours. So why don't we start on our rounds?" She stood up.

"I'd like to begin with the foyer," her uncle said. "It seems to me it needs lightening up."

By the end of their tour it was decided Georgia Bennett Interiors would be given the brief for the refurbishment of the hotel. Robert Mowbray called for a bottle of champagne and they drank a celebratory glass in his office.

"I can't thank you enough, Uncle Robert," Georgia said, her face alight with enthusiasm. "I'll work very hard to make it a great success."

"I have faith in you, Georgie. You're a very clever young woman. You even have a touch of your father in you when it comes to drive."

"I've thought that myself." Georgia looked into the bubbles in her glass. "I can get started on the proposals almost immediately, if you like. We'll need to have a budget."

"Of course." Robert Mowbray nodded matter-of-factly. "It will involve a loan, but I don't foresee a problem. We can't get carried away, though."

"I won't. What I have in mind is imaginative yet practical. Above all, cost-effective. Let me submit a proposal first. I can make estimates along the way. Structural changes cost the most. They have to be done first, and they can be very disruptive."

"Structural changes, Georgie?" Robert Mowbray looked a little alarmed. "What did you have in mind?"

"Well, I didn't say, but a cupola, a giant dome, would transform the lobby."

"I daresay it would, but it might seriously eat into the budget."

"We'd cost it first and then decide. We'd need to consult a structural engineer and an architect."

"We've got one right on the premises," Robert Mowbray reminded her.

"You mean Link?"

Her uncle nodded. "I have it on the best authority he's brilliant. He designed the Lincoln in Perth."

"Gracious!" Georgia fell back in her chair in astonishment. "I didn't even know it was a Robards hotel."

"Lincoln was his mother's maiden name, remember?"

"I know *now*. I didn't then. I haven't been to Perth for years, but someone told me the new hotel is terrific. Strange Link never mentioned it."

"I don't think he's into singing his own praises. By the same token he's wonderfully assured. Secure in the knowledge he's very gifted."

"And doesn't he look it? But what's he doing here? *Really*. I know he *says* he wants peace and quiet. Naturally he'd be observant of his surroundings, but he's taking too great an interest in the layout of the hotel.

He's even asked me how I'd go about refurbishing it if I had the chance.''

"Did he?" Robert Mowbray nibbled his lower lip. "It could be you're a professional, like him. Did you tell him?"

"I told him more than I intended to," Georgia admitted in a rueful voice. "He has that effect on me. He has his own ideas, as well."

"I would think so. I'd be interested to hear them."

"I wonder." Georgia hesitated then plunged on. "Link sees Sunset as an adults-only resort. One central complex servicing beach-front villas. No more than fifty guests at any time."

"Well, it would manage the human impact," Robert Mowbray pointed out fairly. "Not that Dee and I ever let the lure of the dollar override our commitment to the environment. But tourism has grown so fast."

Georgia nodded. "I can see what he's getting at. The island *is* small. It has a beautiful fringing reef to be protected. It's a new concept entirely."

"And one *I* couldn't afford. I don't have the Robards megabucks. I'm not a young man any more, either. I've lost Dee."

"You're not still considering selling, Uncle Robert," Georgia prompted.

Robert Mowbray shook his head. "The hotel is all I know."

"Link hasn't approached you directly?"

"Georgie, I'd *tell* you."

"I'm sorry. Of course you would. But my instinct, like yours, tells me he'd like to acquire it for the chain."

"The price would have to be right," her uncle maintained a little grimly, betraying his fluctuating thoughts. "And that means *high*! The hotel may have become run-down of recent times, but the gardens are Dee's living memorial. They're glorious in a part of the world where dazzling flora is everywhere. Then there's our reef. It's our great draw card."

"I'm positively certain he's taken that into account." Georgia looked at her uncle's worn face, feeling a sharp tug of concern.

"But I'm *not* selling, Georgie. That's the thing. We're refurbishing." Unashamed tears came into his eyes. "Besides, *Dee's* here. She's everywhere on the island. I can *feel* her. Sometimes in the early morning I can even see her moving about the gardens." He blinked hard, then spoke in a more businesslike voice. "We might cut back on the number, though. Sunset has always been family oriented, but there are much bigger islands to cater for their special needs. I'll have to give some serious thought to this. I have to admit to a few concerns of my own."

"What you decide will directly affect our refurbishments," Georgia reminded him gently.

"I know. Bookings are in for the holiday period. After that we could close down for a few months."

"We'd need to," Georgia agreed, "but it would be wonderfully worthwhile."

"I'm sure of it, dear." Rather sadly Robert Mowbray removed his glasses and began to polish them. "You're such a comfort to me, Georgie girl. Dee loved you like her own daughter. She loved your spirit."

"I loved her, too, Uncle Robert." Georgia got up to

hug him and drop a soft kiss on his cheek. "I promise you, we'll do her proud."

Georgia was putting the finishing touches to her appearance when there were several very loud raps on the door. For a moment she was at a total loss. Link had asked her to join him for dinner, but it surely couldn't be he. He had considerably more finesse than that. Besides, they had agreed to meet in the foyer. It wouldn't be her uncle, and she definitely hadn't requested room service. She went to the door and peered through the peephole.

No one. Or a very short person. Possibly her little pal.

Georgia threw open the door, looking downwards.

"Leon, whatever is the matter?" She bent to him, noting the pinched cheeks and the overbright eyes.

"It's Daddy. I can't wake him up."

Georgia's heart lurched violently. "He's asleep, pet?"

"He must be. He's snoring."

"Thank the lord!" Immediately Georgia's fears abated. Adam Caswell really wasn't the best person to be in charge of a small child. "What's that you've got in your hand?" she asked.

"One of Dad's dumbbells." Leon suddenly gave his impish grin. "He does exercises for his hands and arms."

"And that's what you used on my door?"

"I'm sorry." He looked chastened. "I got a bit excited."

"That's okay." Georgia checked to see if any paint had come off the woodwork. It had. "Let's see." She closed her door and took the little boy's hand. "The first thing to do is check on Daddy. See he's all right."

"Why does he sleep so hard?" Leon's valiant little chin quivered.

"I expect its because he's working through all the night hours."

"Yes, on his symphonic poem," Leon confirmed.

"Have you had something to eat?"

"Nothin'!" Leon shook his head.

"Dear, dear." Georgia clicked her tongue. "Next time you could ring room service."

"Could I? That would be great, Georgie!" Leon bucked up, his mind obviously filled with visions of hamburgers and chips.

Adam Caswell came to the door at the third urgent knock, the living, breathing embodiment of a lost-in-a-fog slightly dotty composer. "Good grief!" he said blearily. "Miss Bennett to the rescue again. You're so good. And so patient. I had such a head I had to take a couple of strong painkillers. I'm afraid they knocked me out."

"Leon was really worried about you, Adam." Georgia held tightly to the child's trembling hand.

"I couldn't wake you, Dad."

Adam Caswell sighed deeply. "God, I'm a lousy father."

"Grandpa says Dad is heading for a breakdown," Leon told Georgia, his glossy head cocked to the side.

"Ssh! Grandpa talks too much," Adam Caswell said in a wry voice. "I'm a little run-down, that's all. I expect you know, Miss Bennett, my wife and I are separated."

"Yes. I'm so sorry. Please call me Georgia. It can't be easy for you or Leon. I hope I'm not being presumptuous, but mightn't it be better if you simply forgot your work for a while and enjoyed all the island has to offer? It must be very easy for a creative person like yourself to suffer burnout.''

To both Georgia's and Leon's surprise, Adam swooped suddenly and gave Georgia a grateful kiss on the cheek. "To tell the truth I'm an obsessive personality. Nothing much I can do about it, either. God knows I did try to turn myself into a nine-to-five man for a time. But it didn't work. I'm a night creature. Not for the fun of it. It's the way my brain is.''

"Well, I do know something about it." Georgia smiled. "I work a lot at night myself. I'm very committed, as well.''

"An interior designer!" Adam exclaimed as though it was splendid. "Leon told me. You *would* work with beautiful things. In fact, and I hope you'll take this the right way, I find your golden beauty inspirational. I'm working on a symphonic impression for piano and orchestra.''

"How lovely!" Georgia was becoming more concerned about Leon and his growling tummy. "Sunset should provide you with all the wonderful sights and sounds you need. *Under* the sea is another world. I went scuba diving just this afternoon. It was a wonderful experience. Beautiful beyond belief.''

Adam Caswell's soulful eyes filled with tiny lights. "Under the sea. Of course. Under the sea. A watery kingdom ruled by a beautiful sea goddess. Strictly speaking, your eyes should be green.''

"There are always contact lenses," Georgia joked. "Now, young man, what about your dinner?" She glanced at Leon, pressing his hand in encouragement.

"Can I come with *you*, Georgie?" he asked.

"Perhaps we could all go together?" Adam Caswell suggested.

Georgia shook her head gently. "That would be nice, but I'm having dinner with a friend tonight."

"Perhaps another time," Adam Caswell murmured, a slight flush on his cheeks.

"There's Mr. Robards," Leon cried suddenly, looking towards the stairs.

It was, indeed.

Leon continued to wave, signalling Link to join them. Not that it was necessary. Link was coming on as though he definitely sought an introduction.

"Leon, isn't it?" He smiled at the small boy as he drew close, holding out his hand.

"Leon Caswell, Mr. Robards," Leon said, shaking hands delightedly. "This is my father, Adam Caswell, the pianist and composer. You know Georgie."

"Of course. Good evening, *Georgie*." Link gave her a searing silver glance. "I got a little worried when you were running late."

"My son's fault, I'm afraid," Adam Caswell apologized. "Nice to meet you, Robards."

The two men shook hands. "I'm familiar with your works," Link said pleasantly. "In fact I saw your lyrical drama in Sydney recently. I was highly impressed."

"That's very kind of you." Adam Caswell looked pleased. "It took a great deal out of me."

"Daddy's writing something about the sea," Leon said proudly. "He's going to dedicate it to Georgie."

Georgia caught a startled exclamation in the nick of time, but Link's black eyebrows rose. "Is that so?"

"The things you come up with, Leon," his father protested, looking more like a schoolboy caught out than a heralded composer.

"Then what did you actually *say*, Dad?" Leon flashed him an uncertain look.

"I believe I *said* Miss Bennett is very beautiful."

"Like a goddess of the sea," Leon confirmed owlishly.

"My thoughts exactly." Link was suave. "Now we really *must* go." He turned to the speechless Georgia, taking her arm.

"A pleasure to meet you, Caswell. You, too, Leon."

"Night, Georgie. See you in the morning," Leon called. "I'm going to ring room service."

"He's a bright little kid but he could turn out to be a nuisance," Link murmured when they were well out of earshot.

"He's lonely," Georgia said. "And neglected."

"There are other kids on the island. He'll have to join up with them."

"Of course he will, but he's used to adult company. And he's missing his mother."

"But you're not his mother, Georgia, so don't get carried away."

"It's difficult not to become a little involved. Adam is an intensely self-oriented man. He loves his son, but he tends to forget about him. As far as I can make out, he falls into deep sleeps and Leon can't wake him."

"Maybe he's on drugs," Link said a little harshly.

"Oh, I hope not." Georgia shuddered. "I don't really think so. His eyes looked perfectly all right."

"Look into them, did you?"

"He has a very soulful gaze."

"Well, he's certainly taken with you."

"Except for my eyes."

"What is that supposed to mean?" Link glanced at her, ultra feminine in a full-skirted, strapless white dress embroidered with daisies.

"They should be green."

"Ah!" Link released a sharp sigh. "The sea goddess, of course. Neptune's daughter."

"It appears he sees me that way."

Link steered her into the lounge and towards an empty table. "Someone should tell his wife what's going on," he murmured into her ear as he seated her.

"What's going on?" Georgia responded with such fire three couples turned. "Whatever do you mean?" she demanded more quietly when he was seated opposite her.

His silver eyes glittered. "Georgia, could you deny he's found a new muse?"

Despite herself she flushed. "Don't blame me. I haven't given him the slightest encouragement."

"Look, you don't *have* to. Every time you walk into a room all heads swivel."

"Oh, Link, for heaven's sake!" she said with real annoyance.

He shrugged. "I don't want you to stumble into a complicated situation, that's all. As I recall he dedicated the lyrical drama to his wife."

"You mean you really saw it?" she asked acidly.

"I don't tell lies."

"I bet you do!"

"No more than you. Actually, he's very gifted. But

the whole thing was a bit beyond my musical range. I go for people like Beethoven and Brahms. I'm looking for an actual melody.''

"I practically insist on it," Georgia said.

He lifted a hand to signal the waiter.

"Now what are you going to have, and don't tell me a Perrier water."

"One very dry Spanish sherry. Chilled. I like to keep a clear head." And yet it was hard not to be seduced by his smooth charm, which had a tantalizing bite to it.

They talked of many things, books, films, travel, world politics, a smattering of gossip. Georgia asked after his work, referring to the hotel she had found out he'd designed. In turn he listened with evident interest to her stories of interiors and the various solutions she had come up with. Yet another thing that distinguished him from Gavin, who'd found interior design downright boring. Even his congratulations when she'd won prizes had been fairly grudging. Link Robards, on the other hand, was very much into not only architectural design but interior treatments.

"How would you perk up the restaurant?" he asked, looking around the Hibiscus Room, which had been papered, not so surprisingly, in a bold hibiscus print.

"Let me tell you my news first." Georgia took a last bite of her delicious coconut and lime marinated coral trout, then set down her knife and fork. "Uncle Robert has commissioned me to refurbish the hotel."

"What a very uncle-like thing to do," he said dryly. "It would take a lot of work. I wonder if you know precisely what that entails?"

"So I've never done a hotel before," Georgia fired. "That doesn't mean I don't know how to go about it."

"This is definite, is it?" His face in the golden wash of light was all hard planes and angles. Of a sudden tough enough to remind her forcibly of her father.

"You're darned right. I might even invite you back when we get it all together. Anyhow, thanks for the congratulations."

"Georgia, it's not as though there's very little that needs changing." He looked wryly across the candle-lit table. "Before you start to think in terms of colours, fabrics, whatever, you would have to consider a few structural changes. Your idea about the cupola was good, but your uncle wouldn't want to involve himself in a lot of expense. He would have to stick to a fairly tight budget."

"You've figured that out?" There was a certain urgent challenge in Georgia's voice. A need to assert herself.

"I don't have to. I'm in the business. I know which tourist projects are working and which are running into trouble. I intended to have a word with your uncle myself."

"Ah, now we get to it," she said with deep irony.

"I was going to suggest how he could update the hotel with the minimal outlay and mess," he returned tersely.

"And you think I'd make a mess?" Georgia's voice rose fractionally.

"Really, is there any need to get emotional? You're a professional. I'm sure you've got lots of ability to have achieved what you have, but you need to listen to hard common sense."

"I've got that along with the rest, so don't put me down. I've had a lifetime of that. I know how to stick to a budget. I know how to create atmosphere where there isn't any. It might interest you to know Lennox Larson did the last lot of refurbishments, and they're a big firm."

"They might be—" he shrugged "—but they're essentially conservative. There's no drama in anything they do. They like to play it safe, and many times it works. The only thing I can't see is how they picked that wallpaper." He looked at the wall.

"Dee might have had something to do with it," Georgia confessed. "The hibiscus was *her* flower."

"And they work brilliantly in the garden. Not so well on the walls. The hibiscus motif could have been used in other ways."

"The room should have been painted a pale yellow." Georgia said. "Fabric could have mirrored the garden."

"I agree." He watched her face intently. "It seems to me, Georgia, the way to go is scale the place down."

"So you've said." She drew a little pattern on the tablecloth with a pearly nail.

"Surely you can see my point?"

"Of course I can see it." Georgia lifted her head. "My uncle can see it, but he doesn't have the kind of money to develop a new concept."

"There are partners," Link suggested, as if she should have thought of it.

"Uncle Robert doesn't *want* a partner. This is family."

"Your father is a very rich man."

Her dark eyes froze. "My father's as hard as nails. A

bit like *you*," she tacked on, weighed down by her ambiguous feelings.

"You can't stand constructive criticism?" His voice was tinged with recognition.

"Most of the time, but it seems to me you have an agenda of your own. Whatever it is."

"I'm not about to make your uncle an offer, if that's what you mean. I'm having a holiday and I'm checking out the territory. I don't know whether you're aware of it, but there was quite a bit of talk at one stage that Sunset was going on the market. Only your uncle would have given out that information. It wasn't a rumour that was put about."

Georgia took a quick sip of wine. Her mouth had gone dry. "That would have been after Dee died. Uncle Robert admitted he had thought of selling during a period of deep grief."

"One could scarcely blame him. So many memories crowding in on him day and night."

"He thinks Dee's still here," Georgia said in a husky voice.

"I'm sure her bright spirit still hovers about the place. The gardens she created are breathtakingly beautiful."

"You wouldn't change them then? *If* you had the chance?"

"I'm an architect, remember? I pay homage to beauty wherever I find it. *You're* very beautiful, Georgia."

"And you're a devilish man."

"No-one's perfect." He took her hand, and Georgia's pulse picked up dramatically. "What do you say to a walk on the beach after dinner?"

She turned her face away, unwilling for him to see

her eyes. "What exactly have you in mind?" Seduction by moonlight? A sea breeze blowing, a billion stars reflected in the lagoon, the two of them alone in a world of indigo and silver?

"If you must know I'd very much like to continue our kiss."

Excitement washed her, but she managed to keep her tone light. "Wouldn't that compromise our agreement?"

He laughed, a deep vibrant sound. "I don't think so. I'm not asking for a commitment. Just a civilised kiss."

A cloud of doubt showed itself on her face. Both of them were throwing out banter like bright ribbons, but underneath ran a swift, silent current. One false move and it would whirl her away.

"Georgia?" he prompted. "I'll settle for only one of your thoughts."

She took another sip of her wine. "Wouldn't it be risking your relationship with Tania Harper, as well?"

He studied her with brilliant, faintly hooded eyes. "The fact is I'm committed to no one. You could even say I've never really *connected*."

"As in mind and spirit?" Despite herself her voice turned brittle. He was a stunning man. He was into his thirties. He must have had several relationships. Some serious, surely?

"Exactly. You don't believe me?"

"I'm entitled to have my doubts."

"You think I'm into casual affairs?" His eyes held her. Mesmerized her.

"I can only assure you *I'm* not."

"I'm not, either. Apart from the fact I'm not so inclined, I don't have the time. What's really troubling you, Georgia? You feel safe with me, don't you? You've been relaxed all evening."

She looked at the hand that still held hers lightly. It was strong, lean, clever looking, the nails so clean and beautifully trimmed.

"On one level I have to confess I'm a little wary of you," she said truthfully.

"Surely that needs explaining?"

"Maybe if we were close friends."

"Well, we're off to a good start. I think you know me well enough to confide."

"You wouldn't understand." Georgia withdrew her hand, brushing her fingertips across her forehead.

"Try me. Obviously it's got something to do with your father," he said shrewdly. "I'd say you grew up in a patriarchal environment. Perhaps under a strict domination. You have hang-ups about your mother. I learned that the first day."

"I love my mother." Georgia felt her body go rigid. "I love my father, too but I don't actually *like* him. He's something of a benevolent dictator. Or at least he's benevolent until he's crossed."

Link leaned back in his chair, searching her face. "You surely can't be telling me I seem like *that* to you?"

"It's overreaction, I guess, but you're a dominant man, clever and high mettled. Hard when you have to be. I'm inordinately wary of that."

"When you seem so self-assured yourself? Your own woman?"

"You don't understand. I had to *work* at it. Fight all

the time." She shook her head. "One gets a little torn about in the process."

"Have you spoken to someone about this?" He looked at her from under his strongly marked brows.

"As in psychiatrist?" she joked.

"Psychiatrists are trained to help people with their special problems," he said reasonably.

"I have nothing against them. In fact, I'm all for people going after help. It so happens I can handle my own levels of rage."

"Underwood didn't make you wary?" Link asked crisply.

"Not at all. Our friendship was good up to a point. He was good company, very much into enjoying life."

"Demanding?"

"No more than any other man," Georgia said with some asperity, "but he always did what he was told."

"So there was nothing to worry about."

"Until he started getting jealous."

"There were other men in your life?" Link queried, his expression suave.

"About the same as you," Georgia retorted. "Gavin was miffed I didn't want a *permanent* relationship."

"Hence the ring. If you threw it at me like you threw it at him I wouldn't let you back into my life."

"Really?" She gave a short laugh. "You think I treat men badly?"

"I think you could be the ice goddess. Just how frosted were you with Gavin?"

"We weren't lovers, if that's what you mean," Georgia answered coolly, "not that it's any of your business."

"That's quite true, Georgia." He inclined his head in mock apology. "It's only that I'm trying to get to know you better."

"I'm not exactly sure I know why."

"Let me think." The silvery glance moved slowly over her. "I like *looking* at you. I like *talking* to you. I like the way you're so athletic. I missed that in a lot of women."

"Tania wasn't into three-mile runs, I gather?"

His glance was sharp with amusement. "I know for a fact she always uses the hotel's gym. She's in exceptionally good shape."

"She'd have to be, wouldn't she, in a business where looking good is important."

"I expect so." He consulted the menu. "Do you think we should risk a dessert?"

"Coffee will do me."

"I think you could chance a sliver of orange tart with ginger cream." He glanced up. "After all, a brisk stroll should walk it off."

Far from being a brisk stroll, it turned out to be a slow, enchanting experience, a tropical night's idyll.

The moon illuminated the white beach fringed by towering coconut palms and stands of pandanus that were deeply etched against a sky densely populated with stars. In one of the villas someone was playing a guitar, a haunting, romantic melody, Spanish in origin. It was as much a part of the night as the sound of the breeze that played in and out of thousands of leaves.

The lagoon they walked along was a magical sight. Its surface glowed with a silvery blue luminescence, a marvellous effect of all the sea creatures that gave off a

wondrous phosphorescence. The air was laden with per-
fumes, sweet and bracing, the lovely scents of gardenias,
oleander and white ginger blossom, the incomparable
tang of the wind off the sea.

It tugged at her hair again, launching it into a flying
silk pennant. She put up a hand, but Link beat her to it,
catching up one side and tucking it behind her ear. "This
has been lovely, Georgia," he murmured, "but I can
only resist you for so long."

For a moment her head reeled at the note in his voice.
His hands were locked at her waist, holding her lightly
but firmly. She discovered she was trembling.

"Georgia?" he prompted in a low voice.

Such a shock of desire ran through her she broke away
as though burned.

"You'll have to catch me first!" she called in a kind
of defiance over her shoulder.

"Done."

She had a few yards' start and was very fleet of foot,
fast over short distances but not the stayer he undoubt-
edly would be. Except her heart was pumping violently.
She was running as though from an explosive situation.
Running as though scared of her own sensuality. And in
her twenty-four years only he had unlocked it.

When he caught her she was not only pinned but
swung into his arms. "You seem a bit out of training,"
he taunted her in triumph, not even out of breath.

Her sense of humour reasserted itself. "I never did
figure out how to run on sand."

"I think your own panic let you down."

"Panic about a kiss? I've been kissed a thousand
times."

"Then you know precious few are truly memorable."

"Perhaps." Her voice registered a faint tremor. "Trust my intuition on this, Link. I don't think it's a good idea."

"That brief kiss on the boat was a revelation to me. Of course it could have been a fluke. Aren't you the least bit curious to know?"

"Let me down first." She spoke as calmly as she could. Not easy.

"You might cheat and run away again."

"I'll pay up." *Go on.* Pretend she was playing a game when she wanted him to devour her!

"Splendid! It couldn't be as bad as you think, anyway."

He lowered her to the sand, and when she turned her face to say something moved into kissing her.

It was a moment of molten gold. A brief glimpse into bliss. And it was over almost as soon as it had begun.

She knew she swayed, clutched the lapel of his jacket with her hand, perhaps even moaned. Lord, why not?

"There, that's our little bet discharged." On the other hand, Link spoke in a perfectly calm voice.

"It might be smart not to repeat it." Georgia drew a steadying breath and looked out over the blue-glowing lagoon.

He turned her face to him, cupping her chin. "When it was so memorable, shouldn't we try again?"

In the moonlight his eyes glittered, lending his face a satiric expression.

"You're a dreadful tease," she snapped.

"I'm not teasing at all. I'm trying to persuade you."

"Maybe I prefer things as they are," Georgia said over her wild, knocking heart.

"And maybe you don't. Change *is* inevitable." He drew her into his arms again, lowering his head until his mouth brushed her bare shoulder. "Neptune's daughter. A sea goddess. I can understand how Caswell found his inspiration."

"Don't make me furious, Link," Georgia warned.

"Heaven forbid! You're just a little high-strung. And you taste delicious!" His mouth ascending, trailing little nibbly kisses along the line of her throat, her cheek, moving sideways towards her mouth.

There was not the slightest hint of force, yet Georgia felt powerless. She who had arranged her life so she had herself in sole control. Now her head was swimming with excitement.

"This isn't the seduction scene, is it?" she asked with forced lightness, which was her way of keeping the high sensations down.

"Certainly not," he mocked her, but very gently his mouth covered hers, rendering it sweet and open to his slow exploration.

It was a kiss that had such depth Georgia imagined it touched her soul. It continued for some time, steadily gathering such fire Georgia felt a deep warning start up inside her. It was easy to start something like this, very difficult to stop it. She drew back immediately, tossing her head, but he arched her body still further, kissing the centre of the wildly beating soft hollow at the base of her throat.

"Link?" He let her up, and she leaned against his shoulder, her voice a shaky undertone.

"So this is what it's like to kiss a goddess," he murmured, his glance on her silver-sheened hair. "I'll be damned if it's not the only kiss I've ever known."

Was there the faintest male hostility in his vibrant voice? Woman the eternal temptress. She knew it well. His expression was in shadow while the moon was shining directly on her. "I think we should go back."

"Hey, no argument!" He released her, his tone faintly edgy, yet amused. "A man would do well to fear such pleasure."

"You're not going to blame *me* surely?" she asked.

"For opening the doorway to another world? Why not?"

"Kissing wasn't my idea, remember? Sometimes it can quite destroy a friendship." Georgia charged up the slope, and he came after her with long easy strides. "If you looked into my eyes right now—" she began, whirling to face him.

"I'd *love* to!" He gave a sardonic laugh. "My place?"

"No way!" A kind of rage was on her. She launched herself more determinedly towards firm ground. A minute more and she stumbled across the prop root of one of the pandanus half hidden in the sand. "Damn, damn, damn!" She all but fell flat. He caught her up with cool mastery. "Don't you dare laugh at me." She swung at him, hair flying, like a smiting angel.

"Georgia, I'm *not*! I was only joking. Don't be mad at me. Did you stub your poor toe?"

Inside she was fighting a desperate war. It was quite fabulous to be so enfolded. For a moment she thought it was like being home. She didn't want to pull away.

But she absolutely *had* to. "Probably I've broken it." She bit her lip, her breath rising and falling in genuine agitation.

Immediately his amusement turned to utter concern. "You're not serious?"

"I could find myself hospitalized." There was an odd pleasure in exaggerating.

"What if I take a look at it," he suggested quietly. "My villa's over there. I'm good with injuries."

That set her off again. "I think it's improving." She turned to begin the final ascent, favouring her left foot, which had indeed taken a small jolt.

"Here, lean on me."

"Okay." She looked down and flexed her foot. "Maybe I should have worn boots."

He laughed, the sound attractive and deep in his throat. "I'm driven to say you'd look wonderful in them."

I'm out of control, Georgia thought. *Endlessly, helplessly falling in love.*

There were no words to describe what an utter idiot she was.

He was exquisitely considerate all the way to her room, even carrying her gold sandals dangling from one hand.

"I suppose this puts paid to your early morning run?" There was a teasing look on his face.

She shook her head. "I don't think so. It's not much."

"Then you won't mind if I join you?"

She looked at him and smiled. "If you think you can keep up. It's hard track, not sand."

"I'll call on my mortal reservoir of energies," he assured her. "Didn't your uncle say they called you Atlanta at school?"

She nodded. "I was very popular when I won a lot of ribbons for us at the school sports."

"You must have looked electrifying heading towards the tape. Did you always have long hair?"

She met his astonishing eyes. Felt trapped by them. "Always." Such excitement was dangerous, yet she had never felt so alive in her life.

"Now, you're sure you're all right?" he asked, almost as though he could catch the rapture trembling out of her.

"I'm fine. Thank you, Link, for a lovely evening." Her need was so great she felt like pulling him into her room, but of course she didn't.

"My sentiments exactly." He bent his dynamic head and kissed her briefly on the cheek. "Sleep well. I'll see you in the morning. What time?"

"Why don't we say seven, before it gets too hot? I'll come down past your villa."

He turned, saluted her. "Perfect! Wear a swimsuit so we can take a dip later."

CHAPTER FIVE

IT WAS the start of a week so idyllic Georgia knew in her heart it had to come to an end. The closer she got to Link the more emotional radiation she sustained. His personality was so vivid, so vital, she felt enormously energised just to be with him. They continued their running, swimming, diving, even fishing, getting in so much exercise it was possible to enjoy the wonderful food so lavishly on offer. Australian waters yielded luscious seafood, and the Great Barrier Reef waters, the best. Often they took Leon with them on strolls and reef walks when the tides were right. The little boy seemed to live for these outings, and she quickly realised Link Robards was as fond of children as she was. In fact he told her he adored his two little nieces from his sister Patrice's marriage. His younger sister, Kimberley, was newly married and longed to start a family. His mother had been urging him towards matrimony for some considerable time. It all came out in the course of the days.

Leon, although vastly entertaining, didn't show a lot of promise as a swimmer. His main problem was he disliked ducking his head underwater. But with help from both of them he was making progress. His piano playing, on the other hand, was marvellous for one so young. Enough for Georgia to organise an afternoon concert for any of the guests who wished to come along. First she had to get Adam's permission, but he seemed more amused than actively interested. All his talk was of his budding symphonic work. Georgia had already made sure both he and Leon had daytime access to the baby grand in the Hideaway, the venue for Leon's concert, but there wasn't the slightest indication from Adam he would attend, let alone offer an item or join his son in a duet. He had more serious things on his mind. It was Georgia who thought out a piece for four hands. She had intended to take the more difficult part, but it soon became obvious Leon was more than capable of handling it. It was his concert, after all.

On that particular Friday afternoon Georgia was delighted to see the island nightclub not only well filled, but packed. Even her uncle had made time to attend, but after handing Leon over to her, Adam had returned to his musical labyrinths, a fact that made Link stare at her in disbelief.

"What kind of a father is he?" he demanded.

"He *cares* about him, Link."

"He doesn't care *enough*. I'm getting tired of the way he lies in wait for you, too. Isn't he able to visualize his own sea goddess without fixating on you?"

"It's artistic stimulation, that's all," Georgia pointed out soothingly. "Don't worry about it."

His black brows knotted. "I'm worried he mightn't just be satisfied with *looking*. You don't need that kind of hassle."

Indeed she didn't. What she was trying to do was help Leon, but even that mightn't work out. Leon was now looking on her and Link as honorary aunt and uncle. She didn't mind, but the little boy's life appeared to be so limited he could well miss them when it was time to go home. She badly wanted to talk to Leon's mother. Why was she so neglecting her son? She more than anyone would know just how self-absorbed her husband was. Adam seemed incapable of giving himself, let alone his son, a holiday. He might as well have been on the moon as a beautiful tropical island for all the notice he took of it. Yet paradoxically he was composing a symphonic impression of the sea. An underwater kingdom ruled by a goddess, peopled with fantastic creatures in a glorious environment. All suggesting to Georgia he might have liked to do a little research. But no. He had come to Sunset to prop himself up against a piano while kind-hearted people baby-sat his son.

For a seven-year-old Leon had superb stage presence. He walked to the piano, bowed, settled himself comfortably on the seat to a smiling round of encouragement, but Georgia was certain not a one in the audience with the exception of her and Link had the slightest idea just how gifted Leon was. As concert organiser and fellow performer Georgia sat in the front row flanked by her uncle and Link. Once seated, Leon looked towards her with his beautiful blue eyes and grinned engagingly. She nodded, feeling the nervousness of a parent.

She needn't have. For almost a half hour Leon showed the full range of his powers, present and potential. He had remarkable manual dexterity, surprising strength coming from his bony wrists, but more importantly an amazing musicality and singing tone. He played his party piece, then several pieces composed especially for him by his father.

Their duet at the finish brought the house down. To Georgia's delighted surprise both she and Leon were presented with a beautiful sheaf of flowers gathered with a satin bow. Something she found later Link had organised.

"Excellent, man," another boy, all of eight, wandered up to congratulate Leon. "I never thought much of playing the piano, but that was really cool."

"Someday I'm going to do this for a living," Leon said, grinning.

Afterwards Georgia and Link took him to afternoon tea, where he swooped on chocolate brownies, little cupcakes and mango ice-cream.

"Terrific," he told them, his top lip decorated with sauce.

Link handed him a crisp white napkin. "We're glad you enjoyed it, Leon. But there's not the slightest doubt you'll be sick if you have any more."

"This is simply my best holiday ever!" Leon jumped up and hugged Georgia first, then Link, who held the little boy as though he really cared. For a second Georgia's velvety brown eyes dewed over with tears. It hadn't taken long, but Leon was tugging at their heartstrings. And no one had heard anything from the mother.

They were almost ready to leave when Adam Caswell approached their table, violet shadows under his eyes, a broody expression on his face.

"Well, how did it go?" He slumped into a chair, clearly expecting to be welcomed.

"They *loved* me, Dad." Leon rose to hug him.

"That's splendid, Leon!" Adam's smile had so much warmth, Georgia felt a little more kindly towards him.

"Georgia and I brought the house down with our duet."

"Georgia? Duet?" He looked amazed. "You played one?"

"I *did* tell you, Adam," Georgia said.

"Good lord, I mustn't have been listening. I'd have come down had I known."

"You mean to see Georgia?" Link laughed shortly.

Adam squinted. "I didn't even know Georgia played the piano."

"You do now!" Wickedly Link kissed his fingers.

"You have to tell Dad a couple of times, Georgie," Leon explained earnestly. "When he's working he's really deaf."

"I'm wide awake now, thank you, Leon," Adam said briefly, tossing his ponytail aside.

"And how's the new opus going?" Link asked suavely.

"Oh, fine! Georgia has been a revelation."

"What's a revelation?" Leon stared at Link.

"It's sort of a brainwave," he explained, his expression saturnine. "Divine inspiration. I've been told you've dedicated most of your works to your wife."

Adam turned and waved at a waitress. "I have. But that was in better times," he said sadly. "You're going to join me, aren't you?"

Link looked towards Georgia, his expression sharp. "I think I'll pass."

"You'll keep me company, Georgia, won't you?" Adam begged.

"For a few minutes." Georgia had no wish to be rude.

Link rose to his imposing height and helped Leon from his chair. "Come on, young fella. We'll kick a ball along the beach until Georgia joins us."

"Excellent!" Leon cried, looking as though he was in heaven. "Are you going to join us, Dad?"

"No, son. That's not my scene. It's *awfully* good of you, Link, to befriend my son. Thank you," Adam said.

"Actually he should be learning how to kick a ball with his *father*."

"Well...I'm a real dolt at that sort of thing," Adam said with a rueful smile. "Believe me."

"He is, too," Leon seconded cheerfully.

Georgia tried successfully to catch Link's eye. "Have a good time, you two. I won't be long."

"Fine." Link gave them both a brisk salute and strolled away.

"I don't think Link much approves of me," Adam said, as Link disappeared after Leon.

"I can't really say," Georgia lied.

"He's just the kind of man I've always admired but can never be. He displays all those male qualities both men and women seem to love. I feel a wimp beside him."

"Why should you say that?" Georgia murmured kindly when she was in entire agreement.

"He's very *physical*, isn't he? Very much the athlete and sportsman."

"He's a brilliant architect, as well," Georgia replied a shade dryly.

"Really? I thought he was just in the hotel business."

"He is. He's his father's right-hand man and heir, but he also designs hotels. He designed the new Lincoln in Perth."

Adam stared at her with something like wonder. "How extraordinary! He's never once mentioned it."

"I suppose he's trying to forget business. He's on holiday."

"Are you quite sure of that?" Adam looked at her for a long moment.

"What do you mean?"

"Isn't there a rumour going around Sunset is on the market?"

"You actually *heard* it?"

"Yes, as a matter of fact."

"The hotel is *not* for sale, Adam. My uncle plans on refurbishing it after the season is over."

"That's interesting. You should come into your own there."

"I'd like to think I could help."

"You've been of enormous help to me," Adam said without hesitation. "Not only with Leon but for projecting an image of my central character. It may seem odd to you but I don't have to actually experience these underwater explorations to create an atmosphere in music. I *see* the water. I *hear* the music of the tides. I'm aware of the abundant birdsong, the harmonies of the wind. I can sight brilliantly coloured fish without ever laying my eyes on them. For that matter I can see *you* in the floating draperies of my sea goddess. I have an inner vision."

"Of course you have. Your success as a composer is proof of that. I only wish you'd been present at Leon's concert. He was quite extraordinary."

"Yes, I know." Adam Caswell nodded matter-of-factly. "I was a child prodigy myself."

"Leon's mother must be proud of him." She gave him an encouraging smile.

"She is, indeed. But Liz isn't musical."

"Is that a source of grief between you?"

"Sometimes insurmountable. It didn't seem to matter so much in the old days. But Liz has become increasingly intolerant of my work."

"Perhaps she thinks your music excludes her," Georgia said, taking Liz's part. "Composing must be very demanding."

"Very much so. I often feel drained. Then again I'm a difficult person to live with. I'm not interested in the social scene. Liz is. I'm not terribly into food but Liz adores dining out. I like living out of town. She doesn't. Small wonder she dumped me. She thinks I should take more responsibility for Leon, as well."

By the time Georgia made it down to the beach she felt limp. For a quiet man, Adam's confidences had been vastly outgoing. He was missing his wife more than he liked to let on. In fact, as far as Georgia could see he needed his wife to survive.

Leon, the little victim, was splashing happily in the shallows while Link lay a short distance away keeping an eye on him. Link sat up at Georgia's approach, his eyes moving over her matchless young body in another of her sleek, high-cut swimsuits, this one in a multicoloured design. Her long slender limbs had turned from cream to pale gold. She was wearing a large straw hat and carrying her wrap and towel.

"So you finally made it!" he commented in a dry, laconic tone.

"I couldn't be rude. For Leon's sake."

"Indeed, no." Link stood up, a tawny gold sun god.

"He's a damned sight too high-intensity for me. Here, sit down. I'll spread your towel."

"Hi, Georgie!" Leon called from the water.

"Hi, Leon. Don't move any farther out now."

"I won't." The little boy turned back to splashing.

"And what's with that blessed ponytail?" Link asked in a wry voice. "All that hair. I can't figure it out."

"I think it's called a statement. He hasn't noticed I've had Leon's fringe trimmed. Or bought him a few T-shirts. One gets so involved with children."

Link nodded. "Send him the bill. I'd say he was in good shape dollar wise. Leon's a great kid, but what's going to happen when he goes home? He's become so fond of you."

"He'll forget all about me," Georgia said. "I don't figure in the scheme of things."

"I don't know about that! It seems to me you're landing yourself in one hell of a situation. Caswell needs a muse. His wife appears to have run out of steam. Now it's your turn."

"Don't be absurd," Georgia said a shade uneasily, removing her hat and shaking out her long hair.

"Is it, though? These seemingly weak guys have phenomenal strength when it comes to attaching themselves to hapless females."

"Hapless females!" Georgia's indignant eyes flew to his. "There's nothing hapless about me."

"Don't you think your sense of compassion makes you vulnerable?"

"You've been very kind to Leon yourself."

"But Georgia—" Link flashed her a taut smile "—I'm definitely not Caswell's type."

"Actually he quite admires you. The doer opposed to the dreamer. As for me, I have to say he's becoming a mite importunate."

"So give it to him straight."

"Good lord, what would you suggest? Get lost?"

"A touch crude. You could tell him you're thinking of marrying me."

For an instant the whole world tilted dangerously. "I'm not into telling lies." She had to breathe deeply to control her confusion, a flare of excitement that couldn't be denied.

"Not lies, Georgia. Protection. I think I might do as a likely candidate. Temporarily speaking, of course. We take our careers much too seriously to tie ourselves down to marriage."

"Absolutely!" She just managed to regain her aplomb. "Anyway, I'm only passing inspiration for Adam. It happens all the time, this business of muses. Lagerfeld has Claudia Schiffer. Saint Laurent has someone or other."

"And to top it all off you're a *musician*!" Link continued, scarcely listening.

"I couldn't hold a candle to Leon at his age."

"No need to be *too* modest," he said dryly. "You play extremely well. You love music. You're very knowledgeable about it even if you aren't familiar with Caswell's work."

"Well, he *is* the new wave," Georgia remarked, feeling suddenly tired of Adam Caswell. "And, speaking of waves, I'm going for a swim." She rose to her feet in one fluid movement, long legs gleaming, feet planted firmly in the sand.

"Only for ten minutes," Link warned, glancing up at her. A cool sparkling look with the heat of fire. "I'll give Leon another swimming lesson, then it's *your* turn to baby-sit."

Georgia, busy knotting her long hair, bent to drop a swift, grateful kiss on the top of his head. "You've been terribly good, Link. Don't think I don't appreciate it. When the right woman catches up with you you're going to make a wonderful father."

Unexpectedly he caught her hand, causing a thousand tingles to run up her arm. "Not to mention husband. And *lover*."

"I thought we weren't going to mention husbands," Georgia said softly, holding his glance.

"The right woman can work miracles." His eyes were so bright Georgia felt dizzy. "And who can predict when that miracle is going to happen?"

Who, indeed!

Morning brought a fresh wave of guests. Georgia saw Gavin before she saw anyone else. He was standing at reception, a dashing figure in sand-coloured trousers and a great-looking shirt, chatting up Marianne, the senior receptionist. Marianne was laughing and preening, cheeks flushed, touching her raven-tinted beehive.

Why raven, Georgia wondered. Raven was such a very difficult colour outside Asia. Gavin was a very attractive man, but Georgia had the violent desire to run. She started to backtrack, but as luck would have it he turned and glanced in her direction.

"Darling!"

Every head in the vicinity whipped around. Even Georgia almost held up her palms in surrender.

Gavin broke away from a deflated-looking Marianne to surge towards her, arms outstretched.

Being a barrister had only increased his sense of drama, Georgia thought. The whole thing was too depressing to contemplate. Gavin had come to Sunset to spoil her holiday.

"Darling, how's it going? How are you surviving without me?" He gave her his super confident smile.

How did I start up with you in the first place? Georgia thought, just managing to wipe a grimace from her face.

"What are you doing here, Gavin?" she asked.

He did a theatrical double take. "Honey baby, is that any way to act? How about a kiss first?"

"If I were you, I'd settle for a smile," she said smartly.

"Let's give it a go anyway." Completely self-assured, he wrapped his arms around her, playing out a screen kiss that drew a sprinkling of applause.

What Georgia wanted most of all was to kick him in the shins, but she got the impression everyone, with the possible exception of Marianne, was thrilled for her.

"If you do that again, so help me..."

"Darling, can we go somewhere private where we can talk?" Gavin asked as though she hadn't made one word of protest. He drew her alongside a billowy golden cane, staring warmly into her eyes.

"No," Georgia said as firmly as she could.

"When I've come all this way just to be with you? Hell of a trip, too, but I'm not complaining." He glanced briefly around the lobby, pulled a face. "The place has slipped a bit, hasn't it? Unk ought to let you work on it.''

That hurt. "Gavin, you're such a jerk," she said angrily.

He tut-tutted. "That's not very kind of you, darling."

"I have it from a reliable source."

He ignored that, as well, glancing towards reception. "Listen, I haven't finished checking in. I've got myself one of those beach-front villas. We're going to love it."

Georgia sighed aloud in frustration. "I'm sure *you* will. Leave *me* out of it."

He picked up her hand, kissed the palm. "I love it when you play hard to get. By the way, you look fabulous. You've lost that look of stress. I'm fascinated by the golden tan. It does wonders for your hair and eyes."

"I know," she said flatly.

"But of course! Golden girl. How about a swim as soon as I check in?"

"Sorry." She shook her head. "I just don't feel like it."

"Not you, the mermaid?"

"It's *over*, Gavin."

Something hard came into his blue eyes, giving his face an entirely different look. "That's what *you* say, sweetie. I don't agree."

"Then you'll find out."

"Why, have you replaced me?"

"All too swiftly."

"Really?" He stopped laughing abruptly. "What's his name?"

"None of your business, Gavin."

He gave her a glassy stare. "That's what *you* think.

If you've met another guy you can bet your life I'm more determined. I've never doubted for a minute you and I were going to make a go of it. I've even come around to marriage, if that's what you want. You're a good, old-fashioned girl. I like that.''

Georgia's heart sank. "I'm not a girl, Gavin. I'm a *woman*. What's more, I know my own mind. Enjoy your holiday, by all means. Just don't call on me." She turned on her heel and swept away, only to confront Adam and Leon, wearing identical expressions.

"Who's *that*, Georgie?" Leon's eyes were like saucers.

She shrugged, trying to keep her tone light. "An overexcitable ex-friend."

"Then why did he kiss you like that?" Leon asked, obviously trying to puzzle it out.

"He loves an audience, Leon. I'm sure you can understand that."

"Would you like me to have a word with him, Georgia?" Adam offered astonishingly, like his son troubled by what he had seen.

"Good lord, no. I can handle it."

"Don't like the look of him at all," Adam muttered as though Gavin had been bullying her. "Too flashy."

This from a man who wore his hair well beyond shoulder length. "Honestly, Adam, it's no problem at all," she said, trying to smile brightly.

"If you say so." Adam looked unconvinced. "We thought you looked a bit upset."

She shook her head. "Nothing at all to worry about."

"Right," Adam replied gruffly. "Leon and I were waiting to ask you if you'd lunch with us. We'd like to repay your many kindnesses to both of us. It's been marvellous having the use of the piano in the Hideaway.''

"That was nothing at all, Adam. A pleasure." Georgia reached out and ruffled Leon's hair, watching the anxious expression recede from his beautiful wide eyes. "Lunch would be lovely."

Adam, too, bucked up, but he was still keeping watch on Gavin at reception. "Shall we say one o'clock on the terrace?"

"One o'clock it is," Georgia said with a smile. "I'll look forward to it."

Georgia had barely reached the first floor gallery before Gavin caught her up again. "Listen, Georgia, I had to call in a lot of favours to get a few days off," he said angrily. "Why are you being like this?"

She stared at him. "Why can't you accept our little romance is off?"

"It seemed like a big romance to me."

He looked at her so queerly Georgia shifted uncomfortably.

"I'm sorry, Gavin. I really am. I don't want to hurt you, but I won't be harassed either."

"Harassed?" he cried, sounding genuinely shocked. "It's just *me*. I'm cool. Look, I realise I've made a few mistakes, but damn it all, Georgia, who's perfect? You've got *your* problems, and they haven't helped us, either. All that father-fixation stuff. Sometimes I think you actually *hate* men. And it's all because of your domineering old man. You know what they call him in the city—the mauler."

"Gavin, please." The mauler, that was new to her.

"Don't turn away from me, Georgia," he begged. "I don't think I could bear it."

"Oh, yes, you could." She lifted her chin. "You've survived a string of affairs. If we're naming names, when I first met you you were called loverboy. You'll survive me."

"I don't know." He shook his golden brown head. "I just don't know. You're different. I love you. Doesn't that mean anything at all?"

"It means you don't like losing, Gavin. That's all. Anyway, I told you I've found someone else."

He laughed breezily. "Not that round-shouldered guy with the ponytail and a kid in tow? What an insult."

"Friends of mine," Georgia burst out.

"You're *kidding*! He looks like a nutcase. All he needs is the round wire-rimmed glasses.

"Adam is a highly regarded composer."

"I can imagine." Gavin chortled. "No, it's too silly. I couldn't take *him* seriously at all. I thought I was talking to a girl who liked her guys exuding style, a hundred grand a year, a Merc or a Porsche."

"You've got it all wrong."

"I knew you weren't serious." He leant forward and kissed her cheek, his lips moving towards her mouth.

"Ah, Georgia, I was wondering where you were." A man's vibrant voice echoed down the gallery.

It wasn't going to be the day she had planned. She spun around to see Link walking towards them with that compelling inherent authority, his expression composed, his gaze diamond hard.

"This is the guy. Of course it is!" Gavin muttered. "Now it all adds up."

The two men exchanged glances. Important signals passed between them.

"Link, you don't know Gavin Underwood, do you?" Georgia said hastily, moving a few steps between them. "Link Robards, Gavin."

"Didn't we pass one another at the airport?" Gavin asked, in the awkward position of not having his hand taken.

"Yes," Link said crisply, "as it happens. I've heard a lot about you, Underwood."

Gavin considered that. "From Georgia?" he asked.

"Actually I've watched you in action in a court of law."

"Aha!" Gavin nodded with some satisfaction. "I knew I'd seen you before. Did I win?"

"You got the guilty party off," Link said in mock admiration.

Gavin flushed. "I give my clients the best legal representation I can."

"It must demand a very thick skin."

"I lost my innocence long ago." Gavin shrugged. "When you've seen what I've seen…"

"Gavin is here for a few days' relaxation," Georgia offered swiftly.

"Have you brought a friend with you?" Link asked.

Gavin stared at him. "No. I'm here to see Georgia."

"It was a long way to come."

"Have you any objection?"

Link looked at him coolly. "I'll go along with what Georgia wants."

"Peace," Georgia said instantly.

"It isn't all that easy to find," Link observed languidly.

"Then let's all pray." Georgia's tone was sharp.

"Actually I was more into taking a walk on the beach." Link turned to her. "I was hoping you'd come, too, so I can keep an eye on you."

She took a deep breath, resisting an impulse to retaliate. Keep an eye on her, indeed! "Fine. It's a beautiful day. Give me five minutes." Something had to convince Gavin their relationship was over. "See you, Gavin," she said pleasantly.

"What about lunch?" He looked angry and confused, his shapely mouth twisted.

"Sorry. I'm having lunch with friends. You know, the father and son in the lobby?"

"You can't *want* to," he said with a tight smile.

"She's entitled." Link's drawl had just the faintest edge.

"Then go ahead." Gavin turned, heading for the stairs. "I might do a bit of snorkelling."

"It's a wonderful day for it," Link called. "Isn't life unfair," he observed when Gavin had disappeared on the central staircase. "Just when we were having such a good time. I hope you didn't ask him?"

"Don't be absurd." She met his light glancing gaze.

"Just one question," he said suavely. "You did make it perfectly plain your big romance was over?"

"I certainly did."

"Very wise. I wouldn't want you mixed up with him at all."

"Except *you* don't run my life," she said.

"Georgia, we had a pact, isn't that true?"

"I have to admit I need a *bit* of help," she conceded. "Gavin won't take no for an answer."

"Isn't that awful!" he groaned. "To think a barrister would harass a young woman."

"Don't make too much of it, Link." She heard the steel behind the sarcasm. "You were pretty rough with him."

"Then eventually it will sink in. Incredibly, I heard all about that kiss in the lobby."

"How? Who?" Even to her own ears she sounded on the defensive.

"If you're that interested, it was Adam. He had a kind of Arnie Schwarzenegger look about him, too. He told me some ex-friend of yours had taken advantage of you in the lobby."

"Keep it up," she said, surging ahead.

He caught her up easily with his long legs. "That's how he described it. Leon said people clapped."

"What a pity you missed it," she said acidly.

"I think maybe it was better that way. Even Adam was quite perturbed, in his way. I'd say it was high time his wife arrived."

"No one would be happier than I." Georgia withdrew her door key from the pocket of her skirt and inserted it in the lock.

"Do me a favour, Georgie," he said.

"If I can, *James*." She spun to face him, her heart racing at his nearness.

"Don't be alone with Underwood if you can avoid it." His voice was serious, and he was watching her intently.

"No way he's going to hurt me," she assured him.

"He'd be very sorry about it if he did, but he's not the smooth charmer he looks."

"He's not a closet rapist, either," she protested.

He gave her a look spangled with cynicism. "For heaven's sake, did I suggest that? *Have* you slept with him?"

"I thought we'd settled that. Anyway, it's none of your business." The colour surged beneath her beautiful skin.

"I don't accept that," he said. "Let's go back over our little pact again, shall we?"

"No." Her resistance simply deserted her.

"Is that no, you won't, or no, you didn't sleep with him?"

"Both."

"You just saved his ass, do you know that?"

"Is this a joke?" Her velvety eyes stared up at him.

"No joke. I'm a man who makes seriousness a way of life."

"I think you're a man who likes to talk in riddles."

"That, too." He smiled for a moment. "Now pull on a swimsuit and one of those alluring cover-ups that don't do the job at all. I want to be halfway to the point before Underwood hits the beach."

At lunch Gavin chose a table close by.

He never gives up, Georgia thought, receiving the full force of his begruntled stare. She was considering changing places with Leon so she could present her back to him when two young female guests closed in on Gavin, having spotted him from afar. She heard the taller one, an attractive strawberry blonde in a shrunken top with low-slung pants perched snugly on her hips, ask if he minded if they share. On his mettle, he rose, seated them with a flourish beneath the yellow and white striped umbrella, the girls laughing, excited as though they'd been invited to a party.

Gavin was very good-looking in anyone's language. He never had the slightest difficulty attracting women. Holding onto them was another thing. Not every woman responded to being quizzed about her every movement.

In a radiant mood, Leon smiled at her. "A hamburger and French fries sounds super to me. What are you having, Georgie?"

"Octopus," she joked, although baby octopus with fennel and green olives was indeed on the menu. "On second thoughts, I think I'll settle for chicken breast stuffed with prawns and baked in pastry."

"I'm actually hungry," Adam said, and smiled. "It must be the sea air."

Georgia left it until late afternoon to have her swim, heading out for the pontoon anchored inside the reef. This was the time she did her sunbathing, when the sun's rays were at their most gentle and caressing.

She hadn't been lying there for more than ten minutes when a head popped up beside the pontoon, thoroughly startling her. She hadn't heard anything but the terns and the warm crooning song of the sea.

She sat up quickly, trying to regain her composure.

"Hi, there!" Gavin put his long arms on the pontoon and hoisted himself up, his taut, slender body glistening with sea water. "The things I do for you. I'm a bit out of condition."

He *was* puffing slightly, but he was an excellent swimmer, as Georgia well knew.

She made no protest. Gavin was a guest at the resort. He was entitled to go where he liked.

"That's a great bikini!" He glanced down at her, his eyes following the singing lines of her body, the skin, smooth, golden, lustrous, delightfully on display. "New?"

"Yes, as it happens."

He looked at her narrowly. "For Robards's benefit?"

"Absolutely," she said firmly.

"You better wait until I tell you a few things," he said in a vehement voice, raking his hands through his thick hair.

"Oh, Gavin, please don't spoil the afternoon," she begged. "It's so beautiful. Can't you forget all about me and enjoy your few days off?"

"Sorry, doll. That's asking too much." He gave her a crooked grin.

"What happened to your friends from lunch?"

"I split. I was just filling in time. Come to that, what do you see in that Caswell guy? Hell, I hate those sad, soulful guys. The wimpiest of wimps. And he's married with a kid."

"It's the little boy I like so much. He's been missing his mother. I'm filling in."

"Isn't that sweet?" Gavin said derisively. "You always were a sucker for kids. Don't overdo it, that's all. Wimps like Caswell are good at unloading their responsibilities. Where's the mother, anyway?"

"They're separated."

"I'm not surprised. And what's Robards's story?

What's he doing up here? I wouldn't have thought Sunset was his scene.''

"Oh? Let me tell you, he *loves* it."

"That could only be because he met you. I wouldn't have put it past him to change his plans midair. A high roller like that goes to Hayman or Bedarra or Lizard, like the Prince of Wales, not middle-of-the-road Sunset."

"He wanted privacy. Put that in your report."

Gavin smiled unpleasantly, lowering himself beside her. "If you think *that*, you haven't both oars in the water. You can bet our life it has something to do with business. The rumours have been flying since Dee died. The Robardses move in. They'd probably get Sunset for a good price, do the whole place up and turn it into an exclusive resort."

"It's not like that at all."

"Is that what he's telling you?" Gavin shook his head.

"Yes."

"Then he's just using you, sweetie. The father, Sam, would make your father look like a Scout leader. It's a hard old world out there, and Robards is one big, tough guy. A chip off the old block. I've managed to do some checking. Do you know he's involved with one Tania Harper?"

"No," Georgia said in a low, tight voice.

"Want me to tell you about it?"

"Put it on hold until he asks me to marry him."

"*Marry* him!" Gavin turned on his side to stare at her, his expression absolutely shocked.

"He's a great catch," Georgia went on.

"So am *I*. Admittedly I don't have his kind of money, but I happen to know you're no gold-digger."

"And I've got a rich father to begin with. Don't forget *that*. I'm quite sure it made me more attractive to you."

"Thanks a lot!"

"Gavin, you've never dated anybody who's not what you're pleased to call *somebody*," she scoffed.

"Correct. Anyway, they're always more interesting. Level with me, Georgia, what's *with* you and Robards?"

"I find him fascinating."

"Also I think a womaniser," Gavin said as though such a man should be jailed. "According to my informant he's broken a lot of hearts. I don't want yours to be one of them."

"Thank you, Gavin. I appreciate that." Georgia sat up. "Now I've had enough sun. I must go. Unless you want to race me to the beach?"

"You know I'd beat you."

"No doubt whatsoever, if I gave you a start."

She stood up smoothly, but he caught her around the ankles, holding on. "Georgia, how can you do this to me?" he asked sorrowfully.

"Let go, Gavin."

"How about dinner tonight?"

"I'm sorry, I'm booked."

"All right! If that's the way you want it." He let go of her ankles and sprang up, slender but strong, an inch short of six feet.

"Kiss me."

She stared into his eyes. "Not by choice," she said in a steady voice.

"You used to love it."

"I admit I did find it enjoyable."

"It can be again." He drew her into his arms, holding her smooth, graceful body tightly to him.

"Gavin," she said, aware he was working himself up for a wrestle. "I think you should know Link's swimming towards us."

He laughed shortly. "You're putting me on." Nevertheless he turned his head towards the shore, staring in some wonderment at the powerful male figure slicing through the water with the speed of a shark.

He thought for a moment, then said angrily, "I'll pack up and be on my way. Two's company. Three's a crowd. I get bad vibes from that guy, anyway."

"Maybe that's the way he wants it," Georgia replied, not that Gavin necessarily heard her as his blue-ribbon dive took him deeply underwater.

A few minutes more, and Link rose out of the water like some bronze sea god, springing black hair glistening like ebony, the water falling from his lean, powerful torso. He heaved himself up easily, sitting on the pontoon and staring at her.

"Pardon me if I think you nutty, but why in the world would you isolate yourself out here?"

Georgia sighed and lowered herself beside him, dangling her feet in the sparkling, shifting blues and greens of the water. "All I can say is, I was handling it."

"It didn't look like that to me," he said crisply.

She looked towards the shining beach, the stands of pandanus and the great soaring palms. "You must have been checking us out from the shore?"

"I was, too. I even borrowed a guy's binoculars."

She stared at their legs, his straight and so strong, hers

almost fragile by comparison. "I'm sorry, Link. What should I say? I can't stop Gavin going where he likes on the island. He's a guest."

"I thought your intention was to avoid him." He was looking at her intently, his silvery gaze extraordinary in his tanned face.

"I didn't think he'd swim all the way out here," she said helplessly.

"Your big problem is you're not thinking at all."

"What?" she flared, turning her dark gaze on him.

"So what do you do when he's frantic to make love to you? Scream for help? Between the freshening breeze and the gulls it wouldn't have a lot of carrying power."

"Gavin has more sense than to force himself on me."

He made a kind of disgusted sound in his throat. "Do women ever *learn*? You can't lie around in some tiny bikini that leaves almost nothing to the imagination and think a guy like Underwood is going to keep his head. He's going to be out to prove something. You have to have people around for protection. That's the way it works. Unless Underwood means a whole lot more to you than you claim."

"He doesn't mean anything to me anymore. I keep assuring you of that." She tried to curb her rising agitation. Just to sit beside him, their hands barely touching, was to spark a fiery, sensual current.

"Then this might be the perfect time to prove it."

She turned her head inquiringly, only as their eyes met she forgot what she was going to say.

"A long, passionate kiss would look good," he suggested smoothly. "You can bet your life Underwood will have his sights fixed on the pontoon. Just give him time to get to the shore.''

Georgia blushed. ''I'm not taking part in any charade.''

''Me, neither,'' he said in a dark, mocking voice.

''That's not what *I* hear.''

''Oh, my!'' He gave her a long gleaming stare. ''Why do I have the feeling it was from Underwood?''

''Do you deny you have a few skeletons in the closet?'' she challenged, holding his eyes.

His beautiful mouth quirked. ''What are we talking about here? Hit and runs? I've never dated a woman who doesn't still speak to me.''

''So you and all your ex-girlfriends are one big happy family?''

He laughed a little shortly. ''Put it this way, Georgie, one or two are fairly bitchy to one another. You know, *women.* Now if you look towards the beach you'll see Underwood has finally made it. If he works a little harder he could be a damned good swimmer.''

''But not a tiger shark like you.'' Why was she doing it? Out of sheer bloody-mindedness? He had swum all the way out to her in case she needed help.

''You're getting into dangerous territory, Georgia,'' he warned.

''All right, I'll shut up.''

''Well, there's one way to make sure of it.'' He rose to his feet in one beautifully coordinated movement, drawing her with him as though she weighed no more than a baby. ''And let's make it look good.''

She took a deep breath as if she were about to dive underwater, feeling his mouth come down over hers, covering it completely, the fresh clean taste of apples, salt water.

He kissed her until she was moaning softly, her arms clasped around his powerful body. His skin was like warm velvet, the mat of hair on his chest a delicious friction against the swell of her breasts. She had meant to keep this piece of theatre short, but in the end offered herself up to him like a sunflower to the sun. Even when they fell sideways into the water, their bodies and mouths remained fused, the two of them floating langorously in the blue water.

CHAPTER SIX

THAT evening Georgia chose a plain halter-necked top over a brilliantly patterned sarong skirt to wear to dinner. The aubergine of the top was repeated exactly in one of the floral swirls on the skirt. To add to the South Sea effect she wove a string of pearlescent sea-shells into her hair, forming a diadem. It all worked rather well. Dressing for dinner had become a big thrill, if only for the first moment when Link turned his silver-grey gaze on her.

Tonight her uncle was to join them, but when Georgia met up with the men in the foyer she thought he looked unusually flushed.

"Everything okay?" she asked quietly as they walked towards the dining room.

"Everything's fine, Georgia." He patted her arm. "Don't worry about me."

"But I *do*. You've never had a break. You've done nothing but work."

"Work has been my salvation," Robert Mowbray murmured a shade wearily.

"One can overdo it, Robert," Link pointed out, obviously sharing Georgia's concern. "You should take the opportunity to have a complete break when the renovations get underway."

"Georgia told you her design team will be handling it?" He looked from one to the other.

"Indeed she did." Link glanced at Georgia who was walking between them. "It's a tremendous coup for an up-and-coming young firm."

"She's up to it, Link." Robert Mowbray looked at his niece proudly. "Georgia's a very clever girl with quite a degree of her father's nous."

The maître d' was on hand to meet them. They exchanged nods and smiles with guests at other tables. No sign of Gavin. He was probably brooding over room service or lining up with someone else. The island's three-piece group was playing soothing mood music, and tonight the table linen was the pale yellow Georgia thought most appropriate for the walls, with squat yellow candles glowing from a circlet of creamy, yellow-centred frangipani.

Dinner was a leisurely affair during which Georgia was pleased to see her uncle relaxing. Naturally they discussed the planned renovations. Link, when pressed, came up with options Georgia thought were brilliant. His training far exceeded hers, she was perfectly happy to concede. His answer to her cupola was a new pavilion entry of double height with glass curtain walls framing the breathtaking views of the gardens, the turquoise sea and the distant coral cays. Georgia had no difficulty seeing it in her mind's eye. White marble floor to echo the purity of the coral sands, lots of blue and white for the seating arrangements, one or two accent colours. A few strategically placed marble-topped consoles overhung by Gary Patterson's wonderful tropical paintings. Which reminded her, she would have to contact the artist as soon as possible. Maybe even take a trip to the mainland to arrange a visit to his rain forest home.

As they discussed various aspects of the proposed work, Robert Mowbray sat back, happy to see two clever and stimulating young people in animated conversation. Link was obviously master of his own field, but Georgia had an expertise all her own. It was no surprise to Robert Mowbray his niece had won so many awards. She had her father's business acumen and his sister's great gift for creating a beautiful and imaginative environment, a talent Dawson Bennett took very much for granted. Decoration of any kind was a woman's job, and as such unimportant.

"Between the two of you we're going to come up with some wonderful ideas to revitalise this tired old place," he said, over coffee.

"Keeping a hotel up to scratch isn't plain sailing," Link remarked. "It's an ongoing job."

"Georgia told me of your idea about changing the whole concept." Robert Mowbray took a long swallow of hot liquid.

"It was just that, Robert. An idea. My mind buzzes with them all the time."

"Of course, it would." Robert Mowbray nodded. "Georgie and I applaud the concept, but I have to work within my financial limits. I'm not a young man anymore. I don't have the borrowing power I used to have."

"You've never considered a partner?" Link asked almost casually.

"It's as I told you, Link," Georgia quickly intervened, "this is family."

Her uncle sighed. "I'm past it, I'm afraid. Losing Dee has changed everything. You could say I'm almost at the end of my career in the hotel business. I lack the time and the energy to start over.''

"You wouldn't want to appoint a manager?" Link persisted, his eyes on Robert Mowbray's tired face.

"I'll have to consider it, Link, in a couple of years. Maybe earlier. First we have to make the existing place more attractive. You wouldn't care to act as our architect consultant, would you?"

Link shook his handsome head. "Renovations aren't my thing, Robert. My role is the total concept, and I'm fairly booked up, but I could recommend a very good firm who specialise in structural changes. Georgia would know them—Quadrant Architectural Services.''

Georgia nodded. "They're excellent. As a matter of fact I handled the interior—" She broke off as her uncle leaned forward abruptly, his right hand beneath his jacket clutching at the area around his heart.

"Uncle Robert?" She stared at him in alarm. Link stood up, swiftly seeking out one of the guests, Dr. Lewis, who was dining that evening with his wife. The maître d' joined them, looking upset and flustered, but Georgia scarcely heard a word he was saying. She dropped to her knees, holding onto her uncle's arm. He was quite conscious, indeed he turned to reassure her, but it was obvious he was in pain and a certain state of dread.

Link's strong hands closed over Georgia's shoulders as he drew her to her feet. "It's the doctor, Georgia. We'll get out of his way."

The doctor, a specialist, lost no time making a quick on-the-spot examination before suggesting Robert

Mowbray be moved to his room. The guests were looking upset. No one was eating.

In Robert Mowbray's private suite Dr. Lewis took another look at his patient, who was lying on his bed, looking all of a sudden much older and very vulnerable. The doctor's bag had been brought to him—he never travelled without it—and now he took Robert Mowbray's blood pressure, which was unacceptably high.

"What medication are you on?" the doctor asked, removing his stethoscope and putting it into the bag. It was obvious he expected to hear one of the well-known drugs used to counteract hypertension.

Robert Mowbray supplied him with a trade name from the family of beta blockers, then with a sideways glance at Georgia admitted he'd run out of the prescription and hadn't had it renewed.

"Then you're a prime candidate for a heart attack or a stroke," the doctor told him bluntly. "One can't cease medication abruptly. That's dangerous. I'll give you something for tonight, but tomorrow I'd recommend a trip to the mainland to see your own doctor, who I'm quite sure will want to do a few tests. In my opinion you're suffering from hypertension and an attack of tachycardia, probably stress-related. Did you have alcohol with your meal?"

"Two glasses of Riesling," Robert Mowbray, no drinker, murmured.

"Well, we can't exactly blame that. It would probably relax you more than anything else."

"My uncle lost his wife just over a year ago," Georgia supplied, thinking it central to her uncle's condition. "It was a great blow."

"I see," the doctor said quietly, studying his patient from beneath bushy brows. "Perhaps I could speak to your uncle alone for a few minutes, Miss Bennett?"

"Of course." She nodded and turned to go. "We'll be in the sitting room."

Link, who had been standing by the large plate glass window, turned to face her, his expression sober.

Georgia drew near him, feeling enormously comforted by his presence. "It seems nothing serious, thank God. Hypertension accompanied by a rapid heartbeat."

Link nodded. "That's probably what caused him to panic. The strong heart action. He's okay otherwise?"

"Dr. Lewis wants him to have tests on the mainland." Georgia realized she was clenching her hands. "Tomorrow if possible. He's talking to Uncle Robert now. He was supposed to be taking medication for his condition but he let it slide."

"That wasn't a good idea. Robert's in a low state. I know nothing can cure the source of his pain, but he badly needs a complete break."

"I know." Georgia nibbled on her lip. "Uncle Robert's been trying to keep on top of things, but his energies are at a low ebb. This is a warning, and it could change everything."

Georgia was sitting quietly on the beach staring out at the turquoise lagoon when Link joined her. It was two days later, and Robert Mowbray had received a thorough medical checkup.

"Hi!" Link lowered himself onto the white sand, studying Georgia's deeply pensive expression. "You okay?"

"Sure." She tried to smile.

"Your stillness bothers me."

Georgia clasped her arms around her knees. "I'm all right, Link. I've just been sitting here thinking how dramatically life changes when ill health looms up."

Link nodded gravely, reminded of his father's heart attack. "Not that Robert's actually ill, thank the lord. But it's plain he can't continue the way he's going."

"I should have known." Georgia bit her lip. "I did know."

"Georgia, you have nothing to blame yourself for. Losing one's wife is a tremendous pressure point in life. Robert should have taken a complete break. At least for a time. There's too much emotion, too many reminders."

"Well, he's taking that break now." Georgia sighed. "Doctor's orders. Mamma's got plans for them to spend a month or so at our place in the Blue Mountains. Dad never goes there."

"And what does your father have to say to that?" Link gave her an oblique look.

Georgia shrugged. "Mamma didn't say, but for the first time she sounded like she didn't care. Dad always did do his utmost to keep them apart. Shows what the wrong man can do to families."

"Wrong *person*, please," Link protested. "Women have been known to do a lot of damage to relationships."

"I suppose." Georgia's shoulders shrugged in a kind of despondency. She was more upset than she realised.

"Anyway, I've got a bit of good news for Robert," Link said in his positive way. "I have the right man to step in as manager almost immediately, if Robert gives the okay. His name is Bernie Wilmot. He worked for us for over twenty years before he bought his own country pub, which he's turned over to his son. Bernie would jump at the chance of working up here.''

"That's great," Georgia said without enthusiasm.

"But you don't care?"

"Well, I can kiss off my plans. It seems selfish to be talking about them in the face of Uncle Robert's needs, but what's going to happen about the renovations? They desperately need doing.''

"Maybe the answer is for your uncle to sell."

"To Robards Enterprises?" Her expression turned cynical.

He nodded rather curtly, responding to her tone. "Maybe. We have other options to consider.''

"Oh, don't give me that!" Georgia burst out, her nerves stretched. "Sunset has a beautiful fringing reef. You've always been interested in it, Link. Probably you've been using me to get to my uncle.''

She knew as soon as she said it that it was unforgivable.

His silver eyes froze. "That's a disgusting thing to say, and it smacks of your friend Underwood.''

He was so right. "I'm sorry." Her voice was choked with the effort of saying it. "At least Gavin had enough pride to take himself off home.''

"Hell, yes, after he unloaded a whole lot of malice.''

His face was so taut and angry, Georgia felt the tears spring to her eyes. "It's worked out rather well for you all the same." She tried to get up but he stopped her and pulled her onto the sand.

"Listen, what's really eating you? Can't you tell me?"

"You're hurting me, Link," she said, trying to squirm free.

"You're hurting me, too, dammit. Anyone would think I've engineered all this."

"Well, I do know about manipulative men." She couldn't seem to stop.

"I'm not manipulative at all." He looked at her steadily. "If you've got problems, Georgia, you have to face them down. I can only repeat, I've been on the level from day one."

"Then there's nothing more to be said."

"Georgia, you're not crying?" Very gently he touched her wet lashes.

She blinked furiously. "And if I am? The past two days have been rough."

"Hey, don't you think I know that? Underwood upset you, too, with all his taunts."

"He did have a few things to say I didn't like."

"So how do you figure it?" he asked, eyes intent.

"Jealousy."

"That's for certain," he agreed. "So please don't go putting any labels on me. I'm not into control. I don't need any sweet dumb innocent woman to exploit. I want a woman who can stand on her own two feet. A woman who knows her own worth. You've got so much going for you in every department, yet you appear to believe you're going to make the same mistakes as your mother. Isn't that it?"

"Close." She managed a wry laugh. "I'm drawn to dynamos whether they're good for me or not."

He looked at her, both exasperated and amused. "Why shouldn't one of your so-called dynamos be a good guy?"

"If I find him I'll marry him."

"Then let's keep our fingers crossed." He held her chin and dropped a brief hard kiss on her mouth.

That evening Georgia and her uncle dined quietly in his suite and discussed the future.

"I must do as Link says and appoint a manager." Robert Mowbray stirred his coffee. "I'd dearly love to spend some time with your mother. Even take an overseas trip. This Wilmot chap must be a good man if Link is happy to vouch for him."

"I'm sure he is." Georgia nodded.

"In any event he'll be here next week for an interview."

"You've already decided to see him?"

"I couldn't let the offer go by, Georgie. Not in my position. The doctor insists on a complete change. Anyway Wilmot's only here on trial. Six months before we decide whether the job's going to be permanent or not. The renovations are the bother. They need doing, but I can't take on any more commitments at this time."

"Maybe your best idea, Uncle Robert, would be to sell," Georgia suggested, keeping her sadness well hidden.

Her uncle nodded, as if relieved by her answer. "It seems the best solution. But I've offered *you* the commission to refurbish it. That bothers me."

"Your health and well-being are my top priorities,"

Georgia said firmly. "There are other commissions. You're not to worry about it."

"Life changes overnight, doesn't it?" Her uncle sighed. "I suppose I knew my days on Sunset were numbered when I lost Dee. There's one more thing I was going to ask of you, Georgie." He paused and looked over the balcony at the romantically lit gardens.

"Anything."

"Do you think you can stay on for another week until Wilmot arrives and I can get away?"

"No problem," she said when it wasn't strictly true. "I've kept in touch with the shop. Everything's under control. Mamma said she was coming up for you."

"Insisted on it." Her uncle smiled. "You must have thrown a scare into her, Georgie."

"I simply told her what Dr. Cole had to say," Georgia answered quietly.

"I'll have a word with Link in the morning." Robert Mowbray settled more comfortably into his chair. "Sound him out. For all his gifts, he's such an easy person to talk to." He shot his niece a quick look. "It's a pleasure to see you two together."

"Don't start matchmaking now," Georgia warned.

"But you *are* getting on remarkably well?"

"Link's a remarkable man."

"And I suppose his being here lies at the heart of Gavin's speedy departure?"

Georgia sighed. "Gavin only had a few days, anyway. There was nothing to hold him."

"Just like him, too, to book under a false name," Robert Mowbray said disapprovingly. "I know it was supposed to be a surprise, but really! Gavin's smart and good-looking and all the rest of it, but I never did trust him, Georgie. It's a good thing Link made it so easy for you to get rid of him.''

Within forty-eight hours of their conversation about the possibility of selling, Sam Robards flew into Sunset by helicopter from the mainland accompanied by a very glamorous dark-haired young woman who turned out to be Tania Harper, public relations manager for the Robards Belmont in Sydney.

Link had told Georgia his father would be arriving to make his assessment of the island, but he made no mention of any ex-girlfriend hitching a lift.

It was Leon who spotted the helicopter as it whirred out of a brilliant blue sky.

"Look, Georgie," he cried, leaping up and going into a war dance. "That must be Link's dad."

"Very possibly," Georgia said, shading her eyes.

"So what's the matter?" Leon ran to her, going down on his knees and staring into her face. "Don't you like him?"

"I've never met him, Leon." She smiled into the endearing little face.

"But you don't want him to buy the island?"

"I've been coming here since I was not much older than you."

"But you can *still* come, Georgia. Link will let you."

"I mightn't want to, Leon. This was my special place."

"Yes, I know. I really love it here, too." Leon sank down on the sand, cupping handfuls and letting them go. "I told Mummy when I spoke to her last night."

Georgia looked at him in surprise. "You spoke to her, Leon? I'm so pleased."

"I told her all about you."

"Really? What did you say?" Georgia felt a whisper of concern.

"Oh, I told her how pretty you are. How much fun. I told her how you had my fringe cut so it wouldn't fall into my eyes and how you bought me my T-shirts and gym shoes for walking the reef. I told her about my swimming lessons and how we go everywhere together. I told her all about Link. I told her Daddy is writing his new symphonic poem all about a sea goddess who looks just like you."

"You didn't tell Mummy he thought he might dedicate it to me?" Georgia swallowed.

"Sure." Leon nodded. "I did. We had a long talk. I told her all about the concert and how you and I played a duet. She was so interested in everything I said."

"Did Daddy speak to her, too?" Georgia asked.

"Daddy was taking his nap. Mummy said to say nothing about it."

"The phone call?"

"It's all right, Georgie," Leon reassured her. "She's going to ring again. She said she missed me terribly."

"Of course she does. See how much she loves you?" Georgia moved to squeeze his hand.

"I think she wanted to give Daddy a bit of a fright. I'd hate it if they split up. I know a kid whose parents are divorced. He says it's awful."

"Yes." Georgia nodded, deeply sympathetic to Leon's fears. But sometimes it was even worse if two unhappy people stayed together.

* * *

Lunch was organised out on the terrace. The men rose to their feet at Georgia's approach, and Link made the introductions, keeping a light hand at Georgia's waist. Sam Robards came as something of a surprise. Although handsome in a big, bluff, vaguely rumpled way, with very sharp blue eyes, he was quite without his son's polish. His accent was broad, his manner breezy, the rough diamond her uncle had described, but a man who had battled innumerable obstacles, including a deprived childhood, to get to the top.

Link must have resembled his mother, because there was little physical resemblance so far as Georgia could see. Perhaps something about the heart-catching smile? Tania Harper looked up brightly, glamorous in a turquoise silk shirt with rather too many buttons undone and skin-tight hipsters.

"My son tells me you're in the interior design business, Georgia?" Sam Robards asked, looking at her in a very penetrating but kindly way.

"Georgia Bennett Interiors." She smiled.

"And you're Dawson Bennett's daughter?"

"You're not going to hold that against me?" Her velvet gaze was direct.

Sam Robards gave a great gusty laugh. "Came up against him once and came off the worse. He plays hard, even by my standards. I suppose he gave you a hand to start up your own business?"

"No." Georgia shook her head decisively. "Like the song, I did it my way."

"And you're very beautiful. That's a lot going for you. Beauty and talent."

It was an unusual sort of lunch. Most moments pleasant, others a touch awkward. Although it wasn't discussed, always in the background was the burning question. Did Sam Robards want the hotel? And if he did, was he going to turn into the notoriously tough negotiator right before their eyes? Link kept the conversation going smoothly. It was apparent his father regarded him with great pride mixed with an odd competitiveness, as though Sam Robards envied certain qualities in his own son.

"The coral trout was superb!" Tania Harper half closed her hazel eyes as she savoured her excellent Chardonnay. "In fact, everything's perfect. The view, the food, the wonderful sea air. And discovering such gardens! They're simply glorious."

"My wife's creation," Robert Mowbray told her proudly. "Nothing must ever threaten our gardens."

Sam Robards looked at him for a full minute then nodded as though he totally understood. "If you ask me, Bob, the whole place is full of love. You can breathe it in the air. What say us three guys discuss the island's future after lunch. The girls can toddle off for a swim."

Georgia was silent, quietly simmering. *Toddle off.* It might have been her father talking.

"I don't believe I feel like a swim just yet. Not after that fabulous lunch," Tania said, touching Sam Robards's arm in rather familiar fashion, Georgia thought. "I might have a siesta on the beach and wait for Link."

Georgia was absolutely determined not to look in Link's direction. On the other hand, every time Tania Harper looked at him there was so much steam it was coming out her ears.

"Would you like me to sit in with you, Uncle Robert?" she murmured as their party broke up. "I could be some support."

"That'd suit me, Georgie, but I don't think it's part of Sam's strategy."

"I suppose not. In some ways he reminds me of Dad. Those sharp eyes!"

"I think he's a mite softer than your father." Robert Mowbray smiled. "He idolizes Link. I like that."

"And he's not the only one," Georgia said pointedly.

"No, indeed." Robert Mowbray pushed his glasses up his nose. "Miss Harper would appear to live in high hopes."

"If she does, that makes Link a barefaced liar. He flatly denies any involvement."

"Then if I were you, Georgia, I'd *believe* him. He doesn't strike me as any moral lightweight. You have to remember he must be one of the most eligible young men in the country. One can't blame Miss Harper for trying."

"What's it to me, in any event?" she asked flippantly.

"I'd say an awful lot."

"Maybe you're right." Georgia smiled and kissed her uncle's cheek. "Don't let them steamroller you."

"I won't." He gave her a tight hug. "This is a discussion. I'll make no decision without consulting with you."

As they parted in the foyer Georgia caught sight of Link and Tania Harper having a conversation in one of the seating arrangements near the entrance. It was obvious Tania was a little upset about something. A lover's tiff? Such a fierceness of emotion overcame Georgia she put a hand to her heart. She was aware of an unfamiliar jealousy. Link had made no real commitment. She had fallen in love in this enchanted place. She had no one to blame but herself.

At that moment, as though at a signal, Link looked up. He waved a hand, and Tania Harper turned quickly to see who he was waving at. She was certainly an attractive young woman, Georgia had to admit. Full of confidence, informed, a good communicator, well able to hold her own. Georgia could see she'd be good at her job. Yet Georgia hadn't taken to her. It had little to do with Tania's connection to Link, more a personality thing and her intuitive awareness that beneath Tania's practised charm of manner lurked someone else entirely. Georgia could easily see her as a tough opponent in the game of love. There was no way Georgia was going to intrude, so she returned the wave, keeping it casual. In her room she put through a call to the office before ringing her mother, who had asked for a daily report on her brother's condition. Her mother sounded stronger, more in charge, and Georgia privately mourned the fact it had taken so long. But then, as Link had reminded her, better late than never.

When she came out of the lagoon after a long, relaxing swim, Georgia found Tania Harper in a minuscule red bikini draped on one of the low featherweight recliners guests brought to the beach. Her dark curly hair was pinned into an artful looped arrangement, the expression in her hazel eyes hidden by a pair of expensive designer sunglasses.

"Hi, there!" she called in friendly fashion as Georgia approached. "You're some swimmer."

"Thanks. I love it." Georgia veered off to collect her towel and beach bag before joining the other woman. "I never feel so well as when I'm at the beach. I had a bad case of the flu a while back, but Sunset has worked wonders." Lightly she towelled herself, aware of Tania's close scrutiny. Probably looking for cellulite, the odd spider vein, something like that.

"Sit with me for a while," Tania invited. "This is a *glorious* place! The first time I've ever been here."

"I've been coming since I was a child," Georgia confided, running a wide-toothed comb through her long hair.

"Then you're going to miss it?" Tania flashed her a sympathetic smile.

"It's not a foregone conclusion a sale is in the offing."

Tania made a little scoffing sound. "What Sam Robards wants, Sam Robards gets."

"I wouldn't have thought he was into snap decisions."

"My dear, Link would have told him *plenty*," Tania said, putting a lot of weight into it.

"What are you implying?" Georgia was equally direct. "I understand Link was here for a holiday. Not a fact-finding mission."

This time Tania hooted. "Link's like his father. He's *never* off duty." She gave Georgia a wry glance. "Why, did he tell you that?"

"Absolutely. He said he wanted a quiet, private holiday somewhere he wasn't known."

"And you believed him?"

Georgia shrugged. "Why shouldn't I? It sounds perfectly reasonable."

"I think I'd be a tad more suspicious in your place."

"Maybe I was. At the beginning. But on closer scrutiny Link Robards strikes me as a man of integrity."

"Sounds like you're smitten." Tania gave her a look of jaded amusement.

"Link's an extraordinarily attractive man. I wouldn't have to tell *you* that."

Tania gave a hollow laugh. "I'd be lying in my teeth if I said no. Fact is, Link and I have been on and off for years. We both see other people but we keep coming back to each other. One of these days the whole darn thing has to be resolved. Neither of us is getting any younger."

"So you're not absolutely dropped?"

"No *way*!" Tania replied, banging her palms on the sides of the recliner so strongly it almost collapsed. "Would *you* give up a guy like Link Robards? I'd be mad for him if he didn't have a dime!"

"So you followed him up here?"

"I had some time due to me. It was a sheer fluke I happened to speak to Sam. He was after my boss, but I answered the phone. We got talking. I begged a lift."

"How long have you worked for the Robardses?" Georgia continued her low-key interrogation, keeping calm through all Tania's revelations. She would have to confront them sometime. Preferably when she was in her room where she could scream into the pillow. Though Tania struck her as no novice in the dirty-tricks department.

"I've been with them for the best part of four years."

Tania deliberately yawned. "Not always at the top. My friendship with Link didn't hurt my career one bit. By the way, your uncle is a very nice man."

"Indeed he is. I love him dearly. He wouldn't be thinking of selling at all only he lost his wife just over a year ago."

"So Link told me." Tania scrunched up her dark curls. "I'm so sorry. Weren't you going to handle the hotel's refurbishments?"

Georgia nodded. "We'd made plans."

"How very disappointing for you." Tania sounded sincere.

"It is, in a way," Georgia admitted. "But I care more about my uncle than a job."

"It's a shame all the same. Of course you'll have no chance when the Robardses acquire it. Sam is the big wheeler dealer, but Link has all the say when it comes to architectural concepts and interior design. He's the brilliant creative artist. Not Sam. And Sam knows it."

"So you're saying Link wouldn't consider my firm to handle the job?"

"Hey, Georgia!" Tania held up her hands. "Don't hold it against me. I wouldn't mind giving a talented young firm a go, but Link only works with the top professionals. People like himself."

"You mean you've discussed this?"

"Listen, hotels are my world," Tania said reasonably. "Of course we've discussed it. Link knows I'm very knowledgeable. He appreciates my input."

"I'm sure. By the same token I can't believe he told you Georgia Bennett Interiors couldn't bring the job off."

Tania's smooth forehead creased in a frown. "Look, I really shouldn't be discussing this, Georgia, if you don't mind. I've got a job to protect. I just wanted to warn you. That's all."

"Only I can't decide if it's about the job or Link."

Tania removed her sunglasses for the first time. "Maybe both," she said, the bright glitter of antagonism in her hazel eyes.

CHAPTER SEVEN

GEORGIA lost little time calling on her uncle. He opened the door and ushered her into his private quarters, a faint flush in his cheeks, scarcely able to control his excitement.

"Success?" Georgia asked brightly. She'd been bristling with anxiety. The very last thing she'd wanted was for her uncle to be put through the wringer by a master wheeler dealer.

"Sit down and let me tell you," her uncle urged.

"I'm dying to know."

"It's absolutely amazing." Robert Mowbray took a chair next to her. "I told Sam and Link I was going to speak to you before I gave my decision, but I don't think you're going to have any objection."

"Not me." Georgia shook her head. "What suits you suits me."

"Well, you *are* my heir, Georgia. Whatever I've got goes to you."

"You spend the lot," Georgia said firmly.

"Georgia, I *couldn't*." He named a figure that made Georgia sit straighter.

"Good lord, that's top dollar!" She blinked.

"It is, too." Robert Mowbray rubbed his hands in satisfaction. "I thought I'd start a bit high and come down. The usual old ploy. But they accepted almost at once. I couldn't believe it. I was led to believe Sam Robards was as tough as old boots. I knew Link didn't

157

really want to haggle. He's got heart. But I thought Sam might drive a very hard bargain. After all I'm not in that good a position.''

"How perfectly extraordinary!'' Georgia breathed. "I'm thrilled for you, Uncle Robert. Sad that we've lost Sunset, but we had so many wonderful years. Memories no one can take away from us.''

"But you haven't heard the rest.'' Robert Mowbray looked delightedly into her eyes. "I'm to have my own holiday villa on the island as part of the deal. Link is going to design it for me specially.''

"He said that?'' Georgia leaned forward to grasp her uncle's wrist.

"He said it would give him the greatest pleasure.''

"How exceedingly generous!''

"As far as I'm concerned he has a heart of gold. And that's not all.''

Georgia drew a deep breath. "Listen, I don't think I can take much more.''

"Georgia Bennett Interiors will be asked to submit proposals for the new concept.''

"You're joking!''

"I'm not!'' Robert Mowbray threw back his head and laughed.

"Are you sure you haven't been doing a little haggling yourself?'' Georgia felt a clutch of dismay.

"Well, I did think of it,'' he admitted, "but as it happened I didn't have to say a word. It appears I'm not the only one who believes in you. Link does, too. From what I can make out Sam doesn't interfere in the creative side of things. That's Link's department. I'd say he'll keep you on your toes. There might even be a few clashes, but I'm confident between the two of you you'll come up with something marvellous. Something ideally suited to this environment. You both have a special feel for the place. Anyway, Link will be wanting to talk to you himself. I couldn't resist breaking the good news, though. You are my niece, after all.''

"And Mr. Robards had no objection? He must realise I've had no hotel experience.''

"But it's rather more like separate villas, isn't it, Georgia? Little houses. You'll handle that beautifully. The central complex might be more taxing, but you and Link will be working closely together. It could make you quite a name.''

"Dad might even have to take me seriously," Georgia said, feeling wonderfully elated. Little houses. Little jewels. Each one different. All keeping the magic. Above all, Link believed in her. All their discussions hadn't been for nothing.

"So do I tell them yes?" Robert Mowbray asked gently.

Georgia went to her uncle and embraced him. "I know what selling means to you, Uncle. There's no joy without sadness.''

"No. But life moves on, Georgia. Even if I hadn't lost Dee we'd have had to think of retiring some day. We'd planned a long overseas trip. Now I'll take it with your mother. We were so close when we were young.''

"You will be again. Mamma sounds much stronger in herself. So concerned about you. And you won't be losing your connection with Sunset. We can trust Link to keep all the magic. I'm so excited about *my* role I can scarcely take it in. I've so many ideas flowering in me. At least three distinct proposals, but of course I can't begin on anything until Link comes up with the new concept. It should be an exciting time.''

Robert Mowbray smiled at her enthusiasm. ''Well, you seem to be on the same wavelength in more ways than one,'' he said meaningfully. ''I've total confidence in you both to do what's best for Sunset. I never dreamed it would happen so quickly, that's all.''

That night Georgia put on the prettiest dress she had to celebrate the deal that would make her uncle a rich man, free to travel and without the commitments that had been taking their toll. For her own part she couldn't believe in the good fortune she had learned first from her uncle and expected Link would discuss with her at some point in the evening. The Robards chain wasn't really risking anything. She was young, relatively inexperienced, but to quote the top people in the interior design business she had exceptional talent.

Not only that, she had a career, which she hoped could be successfully combined with marriage and a family. All she needed was the right man. A man who would not only excite her senses but tear at her heart and reside in her soul. A man she had already met. It was possible Link had had a passing affair with Tania. But Link impressed her as a man whose feelings went deep, not a player who entered into one relationship after the other, as Tania had implied. She felt sorry for the young woman, knowing her feelings. Indeed she felt a degree of caution. Some women would stop at nothing to maintain their position.

Her dress for the evening was a perfect showcase for shoulders, an organza halter neck with a small waist and full skirt. The material was beautiful. Pink, apricot and yellow lilies with a tracery of green on a soft cream ground. She'd found herself two perfect pink lilies to wear in her hair, pinning them just behind her ear. The sun had bleached the fine hair around her hairline, grading it with silver gilt. When she was completely ready she slipped into high-heeled pink sandals that were little more than a T bar. It was wonderful island dressing! She felt free to loom romantic, to wear flowers in her hair.

Tania was wearing a red hibiscus centre front of her piled-up dark curls. Pastels weren't her scene, or the soft romantic look. She was far more exuberant, wearing a tight-fitting red silk shantung dress, the skirt well above the knee showing shapely legs, and very chic gold evening sandals.

Sam Robards immediately took charge of Georgia, leading her towards the restaurant. "I expect your uncle's given you the good news?"

"Regarding the sale?" Even now Georgia wanted to make sure there hadn't been some mistake about her commission.

"Certainly, and the part you're going to play?"

Despite herself the blood rushed to Georgia's head. "I'm too thrilled for words, Mr. Robards. And very grateful you've considered me."

"Link's not a bad judge."

"I have no intention of letting him down."

Sam Robards bent his grizzled head closer. "What do you think of my son?" His big, powerful voice was barely above a murmur.

"I admire him immensely," Georgia said carefully.

"Fine. But that wasn't what I asked."

"What *did* you ask, Dad?" Link moved to join them,

his hearing patently acute. Tania and Robert Mowbray trailed by some feet.

"I'm sorry. That's between Georgia and me."

"I'll get it out of her," Link promised, his glance gliding over Georgia's face and pale gold shoulders. "That's if I can ever get the chance."

"So what happened to the midnight stroll on the beach?" his father asked playfully. "This Robards Bennett venture will bring two very clever young people together." He turned his large, handsome head. "Come along, you two," he called to Tania and Robert Mowbray, who lagged behind in conversation. "I'm ready for a celebration. By the way, I thought we'd go game fishing tomorrow, Bob. I spent a bit of time with Lee Mason, the American actor, when he fished the reef. You'll remember him. A great fella."

"As a matter of fact I had to lend him a jacket and tie." Robert Mowbray joined them, leading Tania by the arm. "They wouldn't let him into one of the smart restaurants at Port Douglas."

"Is that a fact!" Sam Robards laughed. "I bet he didn't take too kindly to that."

"Actually he was charming."

Link turned to add a recollection of his own, leaving the two young women momentarily alone.

"That's a beautiful dress," Tania remarked, hazel eyes fixed on Georgia. "I like something with a bit more vitality myself, but I have to say the ladylike look suits you."

"Thank you." Georgia was determined to be pleasant. "You look very fetching yourself."

"I gather congratulations are in order." Tania leaned

closer. "It's a good thing nepotism never goes out of style."

"You can't mean that?" Abruptly Georgia's tone changed.

"Oh, come off it!" Tania glanced quickly at the men. "Don't tell me your uncle didn't make you part of the deal. Not that I blame him. I just wish I had an uncle like that."

"I'm sorry, Tania, but you've got it all wrong," Georgia said firmly, at the same time unnerved.

"My dear, *you're* the one who hasn't got it right. Do you really think Link wants you for the job?"

Georgia considered briefly. "You don't have long to wait. Let's ask him."

"And cause everyone deep embarrassment?" Tania backed off. "Your uncle into the bargain? I daresay he told you you didn't figure in the deal because he wanted you to believe you'd won it on your own."

"What are you saying?" Georgia was feeling like settling this at once.

"Your uncle loves you. That's what. I wish someone cared that much about me. I came from a broken home."

"And you've been trying to break up other homes ever since?"

"Don't spar with me, Georgia," Tania said soberly. "You don't have a chance. Link tells me *everything* that's going on."

There was no time for Georgia to respond. Link finished his story to a burst of laughter then turned, eyes sparkling, to take her arm.

"What were you two whispering about?" he asked her, his expression sharpening as he picked up vibrations.

She had a split second in which to tell him, but decided against it. Not for anything was she going to upset her uncle.

"Georgia?" Link prompted her.

"Tania was saying how much she envied me for landing the job."

"Are you sure?" He spoke in a dry tone.

"Why would you doubt me?"

"You have that look about you," he returned crisply. The air was suddenly electric between them, though they spoke in undertones. "Besides, I've known Tania for years. I know all the signs. She's got her nose out of joint, but she's trying to cover it."

"Maybe she's been led to believe she had more importance in your life?"

"We'll leave that for now." He, in turn, was cool. "Actually I wanted to tell you about our plans myself, but Robert was so thrilled I suppose it was asking too much for him to keep it to himself. He regards you more as a daughter than a niece."

"That's true. I feel I ought to thank you," she added, trying to keep the seeds of doubt buried.

"You bet your life you should." He gave a short laugh.

"I didn't handle that well."

"No."

The maître d' had been watching for them and approached with a smile. He showed them to a table beside the floor-to-ceiling French doors open to the sea breeze and the star-studded night. Once Georgia was seated between Link and her uncle, her eyes dwelt on the table. It had been arranged beautifully with crystal, classic Royal Doulton, silver cutlery and silver candlesticks to enhance the scene. Exquisite dendrobium orchids, pure white with citron-yellow throats, formed a centrepiece, spilling out of an antique silver swan that had long been one of Dee's favourite table decorations.

Georgia turned to catch her uncle's eye. They exchanged a quiet look of understanding. Dee was represented at the table. Dee who had cared so much. Good manners and her own sensitivity demanded that Georgia pull herself together. This was supposed to be a celebration. Her uncle was looking happy and relaxed, and Sam Robards, too, was in high good spirits. The tension lay between Link, Tania and Georgia. It had to be seriously considered Tania had gone out of her way to destroy the feeling of accord. Her vivacious face never stopped smiling, but there was a concealed malevolence somewhere. Georgia was sure of it. Tania was jealous and deeply resentful, but she had the training to keep those feelings carefully under control.

Around them music, conversation, little bursts of laughter eddied. By the time the entrees arrived, oysters, prawns and shellfish prepared in various delicious ways, they had settled into a harmonious group. The food, as usual, was mouth-wateringly delicious, with coral trout, red emperor and succulent lobsters the catch of the day. Only Sam Robards found room for dessert, although Link, ever mindful of his father's heart attack, tried to jolly him out of it. He did in fact cause the order to be changed from a rich chocolate torte to tropical fruit salad with one scoop of ice cream and kiwi fruit coulis.

"He watches me like a hawk," Sam Robards told the others, trying to sound vexed when he was enormously pleased.

"We'd like you around as long as possible, Dad," Link cut in smoothly.

"You think he looks like me?" Sam Robards suddenly demanded of Georgia.

"One can see a resemblance."

"Really?" Sam seemed delighted by the notion, turning to stare at his son's stunning, fine-chiselled face.

"The same heart-catching smile," Georgia said.

Sam Robards went pink with pleasure. "That sounds fine to me, Georgia. His mother's always tried to tell me he has my smile, but when you see her you'll know who he's *really* like. She's a great beauty, right?" He again addressed his son.

Link's expression was indulgent. "She can still walk into a room and bring the conversation to a halt."

"Mrs. Robards is a very glamorous lady," Tania cooed, a trifle the worse for the wine.

They moved out onto the terrace for coffee, sweet, hot and strong. The conversation, which had ranged over many subjects, pleasant and entertaining, now turned to the new concept for the resort. Georgia, totally caught up in the discussion, wasn't sure at what point Tania's bright mood changed. One moment she was making rather frivolous suggestions that clearly irritated Sam, the next she stood up so hastily her chair scraped on the tiles.

"You'll all excuse me, won't you?" she said with a stiff, small smile. "I'm not really part of this. I've had a wonderful evening, but I could do with an early night."

She sounded brisk to the point of being brittle, giving Georgia the dismal feeling she cloaked some deep despair.

All three men were on their feet, and Sam Robards glanced at his watch. "I might call it a night, as well, What time do you reckon we could get away on our fishing trip, Bob?"

"I can organise for seven. If that suits you?"

"Fine. What about you, Link? Are you coming or not?"

"Not this time, Dad."

"Other things on your mind?" Tania gave a rather harsh laugh.

"I intend to walk all over the island," Link said, ignoring her remark.

"Want company?" Tania leaned over the chair.

"It's a field trip, Tania. You'd be happier relaxing on the beach."

"Wow!" she said softly. "Haven't you changed?"

Robert Mowbray solved the awkward moment by taking her arm. "Let me escort you to your room, Tania."

"Thank you, Robert. You're a gentleman." Tania wobbled just a little.

"She's upset about something," Georgia said when she and Link were alone.

"Unlike you, she doesn't stick to two drinks."

"That's rather unkind."

"It's the truth. What is this, the sisterhood thing?"

"I don't like seeing people unravel."

"You're not on your own. Tania shouldn't have come here. Dad should have stopped her."

"I expect she was very persuasive. Anyway, she's a free agent."

"And a born troublemaker," Link said in a laconic voice.

"Surely that would affect her job? She's in the business of public relations, after all."

"It's in her private relationships she likes to stir things up."

"And you've learned at first-hand?"

"I've learned to look out for Tania," Link drawled.

"Why not? You've been on and off for years."

"On and off?" Link gave her a look with a lot of glitter. "What the heck are you talking about, Georgia?"

"One wonders why you're so *angry*, James."

"So call me James. I'll learn to live with it, but I take objection to your implication."

"You're telling me you and Tania were never an item? I have it on good authority."

"I don't think I know what *an item* means."

"Does *lovers* help?"

"What is it you want? A full confession? Whatever happened between us, Georgia, was a long time ago."

"So you *did* have an affair?" Once started Georgia found she couldn't stop. So much for two drinks.

"Sure," Link responded. "It lasted about a week. Around the same time Tania was seeing a guy called Hadley. He was showering her with gifts."

"And you were heartbroken?"

"In a word, no. Tania was trying to move into what she called the big time. So tell me, why are you fretting about Tania?"

"I'm not fretting," Georgia protested. "I'm getting things straight. I have to agree, Tania's a stirrer."

Link fixed his eyes rather broodingly on her face. "So that's what your little discussion was about earlier in the evening?"

Georgia shook her head. "She implied I was given the commission because Uncle Robert forced the issue."

"And your immediate response was to believe her?" Link rose to his feet, grasping her wrist. "Let's get out of here."

"I detest forceful men," Georgia muttered, finding she meant the reverse.

"And who would take any notice of what a woman says?" Link retorted, in a taut voice.

"Well, on the issue of does no mean no, I mean yes."

"Would you mind running that past me again?"

"Link, *where* are we going?" she pleaded.

"To the villa. Where the hell else? It's about the only place I can get you to myself."

Excitement flowed. A great rush of sensation that was fabulous. She couldn't connect such radiance to the doubts that had assailed her. He had only to touch her for her flesh to melt.

The sky was limitless. Glittering with a billion stars, some of such brilliance they flashed tints of sapphire, ruby and gold. The Southern Cross hung above them, the great constellation of Orion, the mighty hunter, with his sparkling jewelled belt. There wasn't a cloud in the gleaming sky, the wind off the water fresh and cool on her heated skin.

Finally it all became too much. With a muted exclamation Link turned her masterfully into his arms. "You care about me, don't you?" His voice was low and urgent.

No answer. Which was a mystery even to Georgia, because she had fallen in love with him at first sight.

"Don't ruin it," Link warned her, giving her a slight shake.

"I won't," she whispered.

"You know you're the only person in this world. The *only* one."

His words were like music inside her head. "I want to believe you with all my heart."

"But you know it. Don't let Tania upset you. Or that nonsense she told you about Robert making you part of the deal. She knows nothing of our affairs."

"It's just that..." She struggled to explain.

"You're a real doubting Thomas, aren't you?" he said in a wry voice.

"I'm afraid of what I *feel* for you, Link. I couldn't bear betrayal. Not from *you*. It would leave me—"

"God, the things you say!" he interrupted. "You're so seemingly confident yet underneath you're so vulnerable."

"I think that happened when God created woman."

"He created the most beautiful creature on earth." His voice was both harsh and tender. He gathered a long coil of her hair and turned her face to his, a pale glimmer in the starlight.

"I *must* have you, Georgia. It's paradise and hell."

She understood *exactly* what he meant, opening her mouth to him and his exquisitely passionately kiss. He was so wonderfully familiar, yet so mysterious. She knew the scent of his skin. It was like some marvellous new aphrodisiac. He was irresistible to her, but at some level she felt a hot curl of panic, as if he could take her beyond herself to some place of dazzling light. A place where there were no guidelines, no borders, only sensual pleasure beyond her most exotic dreams.

When his hand shaped her breast so lovingly, caressingly, his thumb gently exciting the already erect nipple, she tensed slightly. Such a tender gesture, yet it was powerfully erotic, increasing his extraordinary power over her and her yearning, yielding body.

"Come with me, Georgia," he urged her, the faintest tremble in his lean, strong body. "We can't stay here."

Their footsteps fell away soundlessly as they made their way out of the grove of feathery tree ferns and tall golden canes. They were at the short flight of stairs that led to the veranda of his villa. Her hand was wrapped in his, her heart a live, leaping thing in her breast. She was a grown woman, but such desire was as terrifying as it was beautiful. She had only brushed with fire. Now it could devour her.

At first all they saw were shadows. Then one separated itself from the rest.

"I don't know that I can stand this. I don't honestly *know*!" a woman's voice cried out in anguish.

"Good grief, Tania!" Link's urgent passion dissolved into total exasperation. "What the devil are you doing here? Please keep your voice down."

"Didn't I tell you, Georgia?" Tania moved towards the railing, clinging blindly. "He's so *ruthless*."

"Ruthless enough to run you to your room." Link mounted the steps.

"Link!" Georgia went after him, disturbed and dismayed.

"This needn't concern you, Georgia," he told her.

"It should. You've been sleeping with her." Inexplicably, Tania laughed.

"Why don't we take her inside," Georgia suggested as a matter of urgency. "Poor thing. She's had too much to drink."

"I do that occasionally," Tania said.

"What do I want her inside for?" Link demanded, emanating male irritation.

"I wonder if you realise how much your voices are carrying?"

"That's okay," said Tania. "Why shouldn't everyone know?"

"That's it!" Link said, but Georgia pushed Tania inside the door.

"You're sweet, Georgia. Do you know that?" Tania laughed discordantly. "I have to hand it to you. You're one sweet girl." She collapsed onto the sofa in a flurry of legs. "So what do we do now, compare notes? I have to tell you he's the fieriest lover in the whole world. And I'd *know*!"

"Coffee," Georgia said staunchly. "Strong black coffee. It might help."

"They say *not*," Tania commented owlishly.

"What if I leave you two here and go back to the hotel for a stiff drink?" Link asked sarcastically.

"Maybe we could talk about it," Georgia said. "Tania obviously sees herself as a woman wronged."

"We did have a good time, didn't we, Link?" Tania demanded, hazel eyes glassy.

"You think I can remember back that far?"

"I've loved you more than anyone," Tania moaned. "Much, much more than anyone. Beside you no one else counts."

"Coffee, Link," Georgia urged, thinking Tania was about to dissolve into an old-fashioned crying jag.

"It's in the cupboard. Help yourself."

"Listen, I make the coffee, then I'm out of here," Georgia said.

"Then Tania goes with you," Link retorted crisply.

"Throw us *both* out," Tania suggested, almost in triumph. "He's got a cruel streak, Georgia."

"I think I might have, too, in his place," Georgia said. She'd found a six-cup plunger, freshly ground coffee, cups and saucers. She set the electric kettle to boil.

"Isn't this cozy. A ménage à trois." Link pulled out a dining room chair and sat on it back to front. The wind had tousled his hair so that a crisp curl fell onto his dark copper forehead. He looked as highly mettled as a racehorse going into the stalls.

"Got the message, have you?" Tania chortled. "What happened between us, Link, hasn't finished."

"Tania, you're suffering from delusions," he said bluntly.

"Be gentle with her, Link."

"Gentle?" His silver eyes glittered like crystals. "What you don't understand, Georgia, she's revelling in this."

"I *love* him, Georgia. I wouldn't lie to you."

"Here, drink this," Georgia said soothingly, moving over to the sofa and putting the coffee into Tania's hand. "I do believe you, Tania. You love Link, but sadly he doesn't love you."

"He did before *you* turned up," Tania retorted so violently coffee splashed into the saucer.

"That's not true," Georgia continued in a quiet, soothing tone.

"I'll be damned!" Link laughed. "Trust at last."

For once Georgia didn't go for her morning run. She slept late and breakfasted in her room. As might have been expected, once she and Link had walked Tania to the main building and deposited her in her room, their nerves were frayed to the point they had a short, sharp exchange themselves. With emotions so heightened Tania had scored a little victory, after all. Link had stalked off, the very picture of an outflanked outraged male, a bare second before Georgia decided to turn apologetic. It was all so exceedingly foolish. Tania Harper was one of those women with an obsessive streak. If she couldn't have Link herself, she deeply objected to anyone else having him.

That most definitely included Georgia.

Around mid-morning, when Georgia considered Link would be off on his field trip, she decided to venture out of her room, but when she opened her door a woman was standing directly outside. She was blonde, pretty, but so far as Georgia was concerned she had a hostile glitter in her eyes. "Miss Bennett?"

"Yes?" The eyes looked familiar.

"I'm Elizabeth Caswell." She might have been throwing down the gauntlet.

"Why, how lovely to meet you, Mrs. Caswell." Georgia smiled. "This is a surprise!"

"Why do you say that?"

"I beg your pardon?" Georgia looked back wide-eyed.

"Why is it a surprise?"

"I had no idea you were coming up."

Elizabeth Caswell continued to stare at her. "You *are* beautiful. Leon said you were."

"Please don't hold it against me, Mrs. Caswell," Georgia said wryly. "Leon is a delightful little boy. I've so enjoyed his company. Look, why don't we go and have a cup of coffee. We could talk for a while. That's if you're not doing anything else."

"I think that would be a good idea," Elizabeth Caswell said firmly.

They had barely reached the end of the hallway before Link appeared at the top of the stairs. He looked stunningly handsome, full of a crackling energy that reached out for Georgia and warmed her. His diamond gaze swept over both women before he moved to join them, at the last minute gathering Georgia into a one-armed embrace and planting a brief, sizzling kiss on her mouth.

"Morning, darling," he murmured in a deep, sexy voice. "I just wanted to tell you I'm off. I should be back around mid afternoon." He turned his dark head, looking expectantly at Elizabeth Caswell.

Now Elizabeth Caswell appeared bemused. She looked from one to the other with a slight frown between her delicate brows.

Somewhat dazed herself, Georgia made the introductions. That kiss was scorching. Her whole body vibrated.

Link was charming, saying all the right things about Leon and Adam and how they had all enjoyed their holiday acquaintance.

"I was about to ask Miss Bennett—Georgia—if she would join me for coffee," Elizabeth Caswell said in pink-faced confusion. "She's been so kind to Leon. You, too, Mr. Robards. Leon told me. Perhaps one evening when you're free we could all have dinner together?"

"That would be lovely," Link said smoothly, his arm still clasped around Georgia's waist. "Now I must be off. You won't mind if I have a quick word with Georgia, Mrs. Caswell?"

"Why, of course not," Elizabeth said. "In fact,

Georgia, instead of coffee, could we meet for lunch? I actually should get back to my family.''

"I'm sure they're delighted you've arrived." Link smiled. "Georgia and I have never seen such a lost pair!"

Elizabeth Caswell's pretty face lit with radiance. "They *were* thrilled to see me," she confided. "I really shouldn't have left them on their own. Both of them are my babies."

"I'd say Leon was the older," Link muttered as Elizabeth disappeared down the hallway. "At least that got *you* off the hook."

"It's ridiculous," Georgia said. "But I think she thought I was trying to take her husband off her."

"I'd definitely say so," Link confirmed. "See how dangerous it is to get mixed up with married men?"

"It's *too* silly," Georgia protested.

"Yes, but it brought her up here quick smart. All's well that ends well, I say."

"I think she wants them to stay together as a family," Georgia said hopefully.

Link nodded. "They were happy once. They can be again. They'll have to try harder. For Leon's sake."

"If it means anything at all, thank you. The kiss was a great piece of strategy."

"No strategy," he said lightly, "but you can certainly thank me tonight."

"There's one favor I'd like to ask."

"Anything."

"Don't invite Tania," Georgia teased.

"She said she couldn't remember a thing about it. Do you believe it?"

"Nope."

"Me, either. Now I have to step on it. I want to make certain of every inch of this island. You can read over what I've written and look at my sketches when I get back."

"I'm wondering why you don't want me to come." Georgia lifted her velvety eyes to him.

"Georgia, I said I wanted to *work*."

"Really?" She laid a hand against his chest.

"You'd better believe it."

Lunch with the Caswells went off extremely well. With her worst fears banished, Elizabeth set out to be as charming as she knew how. She beamed on her son, constantly clutching his hand and giving it a little squeeze. Spurred on by his wife's warm, relaxed manner and her attentiveness to his every word, Adam showed a surprising wit and charm of his own. Both of them thanked Georgia profusely for being so kind to Leon and both expressed the earnest wish Georgia and Link would dine with them one evening soon. Adam confided his opus was going beautifully, but he intended to put work aside. There was talk of taking a few days' cruise around the many beautiful islands in the region, and if conditions were right visiting the outer reef.

"Isn't it great, Georgie?" Leon said to Georgia later. "They're not going to get a divorce after all."

"That's wonderful, Leon. I couldn't be more pleased for you." Georgia looked affectionately into the beautiful blue eyes. "You're going to need all the support you can get for your brilliant career."

"And we've got to stay friends."

They smacked hands.

With Leon happy and secure with his parents, Georgia decided to make the canoeing trip to Tyron by herself.

As she was approaching the boathouse she met up with Tania, looking attractive in a matching cotton shirt and shorts with a bold floral print.

"Hi, there!" Georgia called pleasantly, wanting an awkward moment over.

"Oh, hello." Tania's voice was light and flat. "Listen, I'm sorry about last night." She stood in front of Georgia, almost blocking her way.

"It's forgotten," Georgia fibbed. "I don't like to see anyone upset."

"It was all true, you know." Tania's hazel eyes were dark and stormy.

"Tania!" Georgia held up a staying hand. "I don't want to discuss this further."

"You'd be wise to listen. Link is Sam Robards's heir and his mother's adored only son. There's not a woman alive good enough for him. Just wait until you meet her."

"Whether I meet her or not remains to be seen," Georgia said.

"You want Link, don't you?" Tania asked sharply.

"This is all private, Tania. I'm sorry." Georgia made to pass.

"Well, best of luck." Tania stood aside with an ironic salute. "Trying to hold onto a guy like Link is like trying to catch a tiger by the tail. Who knows, you might be like me and get badly mauled."

It was delivered like a parting salvo, and it found its mark. As much as she knew Tania was deeply jealous, the whole situation took the shine off Georgia's day. It was just as well the new manager was arriving, and she and Uncle Robert could get away.

By the time she reached the cay she was almost out of breath. For once the crossing had been like scaling a mountain, and she put it down to the fact Tania had upset her. She was human, after all, and very much in love. It seemed incredible to her her life had taken such an overwhelming change. It was difficult to deal with the suddenness and intensity of feeling.

Link had cut into her most profound being, but along with the wonder and desire there were needs and fears to be settled. She realized the traumas of childhood and adolescence still affected her. The old worry she might somehow be drawn to a man who would only make her suffer. Her mother had married such a man. It could be argued she was much stronger than her mother, much more independent, that Link bore no resemblance to her father beyond a certain male toughness. What she had to do was abandon the old emotional freight, to feel secure enough to totally let go.

Puffing a little, she pulled the canoe onto the shingle. She was looking forward to a quick cooling dip. How lovely it was here. The water looked wonderful, a jewel-like aquamarine. Several species of birds had their breeding grounds on Tyron. She watched as the gregarious little noddies and silver gulls came down to greet her, unconcerned by her presence. Green turtles also bred on the cay. A short distance away was the track where one of them had used its curious rowing action to slide into the water.

Years ago Dee had planted a line of coconut palms, and now Georgia sought their shade. One of them had been bent to an angle of forty-five degrees by the prevailing winds, and she leaned against it getting her breath. The vegetation on the cay was even more luxuriant than she remembered, thicker stands of pandanus with their prop roots and pineapple-like fruit, the taller pisonias with large pale green leaves, the feathery casuarinas. Long ribbons of yellow-flowering succulents decorated the low dunes and ran down onto the strand, their faces as bright as daisies. The view back to Sunset was beautiful, the shadings in the water incredible, the distinct tones as clearly defined as lines drawn across a painting. The light was so clear, so bright the horizon seemed to run on forever. How she loved her Treasure Island with all its memories.

After her swim Georgia visited all the old spots that were so special to her, gathering a few prettily marked shells for Leon before lying down in the shade. As always these days her thoughts turned to Link. Their relationship had moved with the speed of a lightning bolt. The *coup de foudre* of fiction. Except it really *had* happened. There had been no opportunity to ask her uncle if he had interceded on her behalf for the interior design commission. Now she decided she wouldn't. Who was she to trust, after all? Two men she loved, or foxy Tania Harper who had an agenda all her own?

Her mind tired, feeling faintly dizzy, Georgia dozed off. When she awoke some forty minutes later she realized the tide was coming in fast. It would be wise to paddle back now. She stood up quickly, but as she did so she reeled abruptly then fell back on the sand.

Vertigo. She suffered from it now and then, especially if she'd been diving. The only good thing was the sensation quickly passed.

Except this time it didn't. Georgia gave it a few

minutes more, then tried to rise. Her head spun like a top. She felt a wave of nausea that had her lying prone. Keep calm, she thought. This will pass. It always does. She just needed stillness.

When Link returned to the hotel Georgia was nowhere to be found. She couldn't be on the beach. The sunset had come and gone in a blaze of glory, and the stars were coming out in their hundreds of thousands. No one at reception knew where she was. He spotted Tania in the lounge, enjoying a drink with a male guest. Trust Tania, he thought. He approached their table, asking if Tania had any idea where Georgia might be.

"Sorry." Tania looked up casually. "I met up with her once this afternoon. As far as I know she was just going down to the beach." She could have said *boathouse*, but why make it easy? Let him suffer. Under that controlled, super-confident facade she would have sworn Link Robards was fairly frantic.

It was Leon who remembered Georgia had said she was going over to Tryon. "She was going to take me, only Mummy arrived," he told Link. "Anyway, Miss Harper would know. They were talking near the boathouse. I saw them."

Link's face turned grim. He would follow up *that* piece of information later. He moved fast, taking out the dinghy he and Georgia used on their scuba diving expeditions, pointing it westward across the warm, sheltered waters. He couldn't think beyond getting to Tryon. Finding her. This was the worst dread he had ever known, yet he clung to the fact she was an excellent swimmer. She handled a boat extremely well. He stared towards the adjacent cay, a dark silhouette against the radiant sky. A full moon rode high, exceptionally big and luminous, laying down a track like a silver blaze between the two islands. His vision was sharp, fully focused, his body full of power from the charge of adrenaline. Once he hit a current. The small craft rocked, then moved steadily forwards. The lights of Sunset were behind him. He could see nothing ahead but darkness against a pearlescent sky.

Nearing the beach, he felt a sudden intense fear. What if she weren't there? What if Leon had got it wrong? She hadn't gone diving. He had checked that out. Tryon was as close as he could get to solving the mystery. Georgia had often spoken about visiting the coral cay. She had wanted to take Leon, let him explore.

It was some comfort to realise she knew the cay well. There were no high places from which she could fall. No snakes. No venomous animals. The only threat came from the sea. Shark attacks were rarely heard of in these waters. There was the odd horror story about the worst scorpion fish, the stone fish, but all scorpion fish were sluggish bottom dwellers, living among the seaweed and coral rubble. Cone shells had caused serious injuries in the past but Georgia would know all about them. She had grown up in this world.

He beached the dinghy and looked around for some sign of a boat, some sign of life. There was a great knot inside him that was tightening its grip. He was gritting his teeth silently against the boundless anxiety.

He began to call her name, his voice amazingly clear on the still air. More than anything in the world he wanted to see her, to hold her, to assure himself of her safety.

There was a vague rustling from the line of trees. Just

the singing of the leaves. Then she came at him like a gazelle. Her blonde hair flowed like a banner on the breeze. Her long, bare legs gleamed dully in the silvery light. He felt electrified, his mood suddenly turbulent. He ran to meet her, taking her roughly in his arms, kissing her, crushing her to him.

"What the devil do you mean giving me a fright like that?"

Such an extraordinary thing to hear the violence in his voice, but fear hadn't vanished without a trace. She felt small in his arms, slender, yet womanly, curved. Her own special fragrance clung to her. Clung to him.

"Link!" She rested her head against his chest, her long hair veiling her profile. "I'm so sorry you were worried."

"Worried?" He let out a long, whistling sigh. "I was nearly off my head."

"I had an attack of vertigo," she explained.

"Good God!" He held her away from him and stared into the pale oval of her face. "How are you now?"

"All right. The attack passed more than an hour ago. *After* the tide came in and collected my canoe. I couldn't stop it. I couldn't get it. I had to watch it float away."

"Why did you *do* this?" he groaned. "Why did you go by yourself?"

"I wasn't in any danger. There's nothing on the island to hurt me. I just had to sit it out. Besides, I had the certainty you'd come for me."

"To the ends of the earth," he said with a harshness born of emotion.

"You must love me."

"Beyond anything." He spoke with deep conviction.

"I see such a future for us, Georgia. The promise of developing our careers together. I see children. A family."

"A *home*. Belonging," Georgia added shakily.

He kissed her forehead, her eyes, finally her mouth, feeling it open to him like an unfurling rose. "Georgia, they're not tears?" He caught a crystal drop on his tongue.

"It's perfectly normal for a woman to cry with happiness," she breathed.

"Where have you been all my life?"

"Waiting for you."

"No doubts?"

"None." A tide of emotion surged through her. "I'm fiercely proud of you. I love you." She lifted on tiptoes, making pecking little kisses all over his face.

"And I'll cherish you for the rest of your life." He bent to kiss her. "It would be *so* wonderful to stay here, but I must take you back. Everyone will be worrying about us."

"Yes, I know." Georgia clasped his hand, feeling such buoyancy she thought she could float back to Sunset. "I'm not dreaming all this, am I?"

"It's like a dream to me, too." He gave a deep elated laugh. "In fact I was beginning to wonder if I'd ever find my one perfect mate. The missing piece of my soul."

"We'll come back here, won't we?" Georgia asked.

"You *know* we will." He took her hand and kissed it. "This is where we declared our love."

EPILOGUE

Christmas Eve, eighteen months later

THE Christmas tree lofted almost to the high ceiling, festooned with the most beautiful ornaments Georgia could find, scarlet and green baubles, tiny boxes and drums lavishly decorated, sugary white and gold Christmas bells, heralding little angels in fine bisque porcelain dancing on golden threads, each winged cherub playing a different musical instrument. Sparkling tinsel cast a bright illumination, and dozens of fairy lights silhouetted each individual branch, causing the baubles to shimmer and glow and throw back a kaleidoscope of colours. At the very top of the tree was the glittering start of Bethlehem, the permanent symbol of peace, and just beneath it Noel, the angel of Christmas, with her exquisite porcelain face and rich raiment in the glorious colours of Christmas, ruby red and emerald trimmed with gold lamé to match her outstretched wings. The presents were piled high beneath the tree, as luxuriously wrapped and beribboned as Georgia knew how. She and Link had had a marvellous time decorating the tree, the house filled with their happy laughter and the golden voice of Dame Kiri Te Kanawa singing their favourite carols.

Looking around the beautiful home Link had designed and built for her, Georgia felt such an overflow of joy the tears rose to her eyes. This was a timeless moment. Soft and gleaming. A perfect moment in life when all

185

her dreams were fulfilled. She would hold onto it for all time. The long skirt of her dress rustled as she began to move from living to dining room and out onto the plant-filled terrace that overlooked the fairytale glitter of night-time Sydney Harbour.

Her dress had been made from a gorgeous piece of green and gold embroidered silk her mother-in-law had given her. It seemed so right for Christmas. In the past year of her marriage she and Kate had become very close. Indeed, she had come to accept with gratitude Kate and Sam were far more caring, more involved and supportive than ever her parents were. It wasn't what she wanted, but it was the way her life had turned out. It was Kate who showed tremendous interest in Georgia's career. Kate who'd been so delighted with Georgia's total design concept for Sunset, travelling back and forth with Georgia as they made frequent trips to the island.

The new Sunset had reopened to considerable fanfare in late September, with extensive magazine coverage for Link and herself. It had been a breathless, scintillating time, her life in top gear, not without a few hassles and differences of opinion but with the give-and-take that was to characterise them. She and Link had always arrived at solutions that pleased them and eventually everyone else. Georgia was immensely proud of her husband. She felt she had blossomed under the warmth and brilliance of his influence.

They were supremely happy, and for that she thanked God every night of her life. It was with great joy and pride she carried their child, the greatest blessing a loving married couple could ever know. Her pregnancy had only just been confirmed.

She and Link had decided to announce their splendid news at midnight, when all the family was assembled. Kate and Sam would be thrilled out of their minds. They were intensely *family* people. Georgia's mother would be delighted. She thought her father would be happy, too. His first grandchild. There would be immediate talk of which schools *he* would go to. She and Link wanted no advance knowledge of the sex of their child. They were happy to wait for their wonderful little surprise package.

The house was filled with Christmas lilies, with great crystal bowls of her favourite long-stemmed red roses. She had even managed to find the time to make a decorative swag for the white marble mantelpiece, the dark evergreen foliage decorated with sumptuous little trinkets. It had been the greatest fun. She loved the graceful things in life. Even the standard ficus that stood in stone pots to flank the front door she had decorated with red and gold bows. Christmas wasn't just a festive season to her. Christmas really *meant* something. She touched a hand to her still flat stomach. Next Christmas, with the grace of God, she and Link would have their first beloved child. It was time of high emotion.

In another few minutes Link would join her. He had been delayed in town and had to rush to shower and dress. Tonight was for family. There would be around twenty at their celebration buffet. The hired trestle looked marvellous draped with dark green damask, golden tassels sweeping the parqueted floor of the dining room. She had used bright red highly polished apples for a centrepiece, interspersing the fruit with glossy camellia leaves. She thought it looked very effective surrounded by silver platters of smoked salmon rolls filled with a blend of crabmeat cream cheese and mayonnaise, lobster medallions, prawn barquettes and quail eggs, caviar and cream cheese on pastry, turkey and glazed ham, stuffed mushrooms, jubilee eggs with pesto. The two hot dishes, one beef, the other chicken sitting on a bed of rice, were in the kitchen waiting for gentle reheating. Three desserts were offered. A snowball of plum pudding, a magnificent chocolate log piled high with a chocolate caraque and served with crème chantilly, and especially for Sam a fresh fruit tart with the fruit arranged in concentric circles on a vanilla pastry cream.

They had planned a New Year's party for their friends and all the people who had been so supportive on the Sunset project. Uncle Robert was still abroad. He had met up with an old school chum in Moscow, of all places. The two of them intended to take in a few of the major European art galleries. Georgia would be speaking to him some time Christmas morning. She knew it would be emotional, what with all her news. That would bring him home.

"Darling?" Link's dark head appeared over the gleaming banister of the gallery. He was fully dressed in black tie—they wanted to make of it a memorable occasion—so heartbreakingly handsome, so *dear*, she had the wonderful sensation of bright light within her.

It showed in her upturned face. "Oh, you're dressed," she exclaimed radiantly. "That's good. They should be here soon."

"Not before I've given you my Christmas present. I'd like you to wear it."

"What is it? Tell me." Link had never stopped showering her with presents, but she still got excited.

"Don't you *dare* run up the stairs." He met her halfway, slipping an arm around her waist. "You're everything in the world to me, and don't you forget it."

She leaned her head against his shoulder. "And you to me, my love. You're so good to me when we've got the greatest Christmas gift we could ever wish for."

"That we have." He dropped a fervent kiss on the top of her shining head.

In their bedroom, Link slipped a pendant necklace around his wife's slender throat, holding her shoulders while they both studied the effect.

"It's absolutely lovely!" Georgia touched a hand to the pendant suspended from a gleaming gold chain. It was a beautifully designed sunburst in gold, at the centre a fully faceted Burmese ruby that seemed to glow with a life of its own. It complemented her skin and her dress perfectly.

"I designed it and had it made up. Gold for our happiness. Red for our love." He turned her to him, taking her face gently between his elegant hands. "This has been the most fulfilling year of my life, Georgia. Thank you with all my heart."

"And it's going to get better," Georgia promised, her dark eyes lustrous with the depth of her emotions.

They had barely arrived downstairs before the door chimes rang through the house.

"That's the family," Link said, in his vibrant voice. He took her hand as they walked down the hallway and opened the door on a cluster of bright, smiling faces.

He and Georgia stood silhouetted, hands clasped, their bodies leaning in to each other. In unity. The two of them. Three, really. Inside of Georgia a tiny heart was beating strongly.

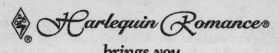

brings you

Authors you'll treasure,
books you'll want to keep!

Harlequin Romance just keeps getting better and
better...and we're delighted to welcome you to our
Simply the Best showcase for 1997, highlighting a
special author each month!

These are stories we know you'll love reading—again
and again! Because they are, quite simply, the best...

Don't miss these unforgettable romances coming to you
in May, June and July.

May—GEORGIA AND THE TYCOON (#3455)
by Margaret Way
June—WITH HIS RING (#3459)
by Jessica Steele
July—BREAKFAST IN BED (#3465)
by Ruth Jean Dale

Available wherever Harlequin books are sold.

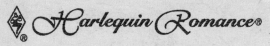

Harlequin Romance®

**is proud to announce the latest arrivals
in our bouncing baby series**

Each month in 1997 we'll be bringing you your very
own bundle of joy—a cute, delightful romance by
one of your favorite authors. Our heroes and heroines
are about to discover that two's company and three
(or four...or five) is a family!

Find out about the true labor of love...

Don't miss these charming stories
of parenthood, and how to survive it,
coming in May, June and July.

**May—THE SECRET BABY (#3457)
by Day Leclaire
June—FOR BABY'S SAKE (#3461)
by Val Daniels
July—BABY, YOU'RE MINE! (#3463)
by Leigh Michaels**

Available wherever Harlequin books are sold.

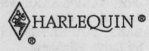